Lock Down Publications and Ca$h
Presents

I0564753

RELENTLESS GOON

Power Moves of a Real One

Written By
Prince A. Tauhid

First Edition 2024

Printed in the United States of America

This is a work of fiction. Names, characters, places, and incidents either
are products of the author's imagination or are used fictitiously. Any
similarity to actual events or locales or persons, living or dead, is
entirely coincidental.

Lock Down Publications
P.O. Box 944
Stockbridge, GA 30281
www.lockdownpublications.com

Like our page on Facebook: Lock Down Publications
www.facebook.com/lockdownpublications.ldp

Stay Connected with Us!

Text **LOCKDOWN** to 22828 to stay up-to-date with new releases, sneak peaks, contests and more…

Like our page on Facebook:
Lock Down Publications

Join Lock Down Publications/The New Era Reading Group

Visit our website:
www.lockdownpublications.com

Follow us on Instagram:
Lock Down Publications

Email Us: We want to hear from you!

PROLOGUE

Three Years Earlier . . .

At the FBI Headquarters in Washington DC, the Director and his team of men and women were holding a briefing regarding the influx of military grade weapons and large quantities of hard drugs that had flooded the streets of Miami Florida. Numerous reports were provided from the field office there of the criminal enterprises that was solely responsible for the narcotics, and there were possible leads regarding the lethal weapons.

Before the day of the meeting, many conventional methods had been used in an attempt to penetrate the organization headed by a Raymond Eugene Stephens and his associates, most notable, a Mitchell Duvalier-Collins, the second in command. All to no avail. Therefore, the Bureau needed to come up with something more effective if they truly intended to take down this particular crew of hard knocks.

The topics regarding the lead person pushing the firearms and ammunition through the *"Iron Pipeline" was* many and far in between. Multiple briefings took place. They had a person of interest to start with. And if all was to go well with him, this would ensure that the door would be cracked for further insight into the operation.

The Director; a Dean Windsor, opened up by giving instructions on how they were to go about pursuing their targets.

"Greetings my dear people. Glad to have you all here. As you may know, the reason for this particular meeting is very simple to understand. We have a couple of bad guys on our hand that seems to be hard to touch, for the most part, but not so entirely. So, what we're here today for is this. We're gonna need to plant someone inside of this enterprise to get as close as possible to our primary target, then from there, the take down could proceed," Windsor stated.

He continued, "without running down the complete history of the subject of this investigation that we're gonna name 'Operation Ghost Member,' so as to arrest our target Raymond Eugene Stephens, I give you this much . . . ."

The Director then chronologically recited the history of the target Stephens; that of his top associate; how Stephens inherited the drug empire he ran with an iron fist (according to the knowledge and info which they had); years of recorded documentation of audio tapes and written reports related about the brother of Stephens—a Phillip Theodore Stephens—and all other materials necessary to help paint a better picture of the criminals they were dealing with.

"So, now that I have laid it all out for you on the direction we're to take in this relaunch operation, I'm now gonna appoint a designated person whom is to penetrate the ranks of this crew, and temporarily become one of them. You there," he pointed to a well trained agent that was qualified for the mission at hand, "would you be willing to accept the responsibility I now place upon you to do the work which lies ahead?" Windsor asked.

The young ambitious agent spoke up. "Why ah . . . yes . . . I will. That's what I signed up to be an FBI agent for. To take down the bad guys," the now Federal mole declared, gladly taking on the assignment.

"Perfect! You are absolutely perfect for the job. Also, to our knowledge, there is a connection between the drugs and the guns that heavily saturate Miami-Dade, Florida Once we're able to get one up and the process going, it shall open the door for the next, and we'll essentially be able to take out two operations through one medium. You all got that? This meeting is adjourned," Windsor concluded.

—

Presently . . .

The cousin of a Miami native and relentless street gangster, a Melvin Anderson aka "Parlay," was a dude by the name Vick. He'd been told by Parlay himself that he would be getting out of prison in the next two weeks. Vick hadn't long made strategic power moves to put him over the million dollar mark in the game he played in on the streets. He had bossed up and was really doing his thing. He wanted to celebrate his success and also to honor his cousin's return home at the hottest strip club all the south, possibly the country, *King Of Dimez* Gentlemen Night Club there in Miami.

He'd bought out the bar, and him and his crew popped bottles, smoked blunts, expensive cigars, and had all the fine girls up in there breaking their necks trying to pick up that cash them niggaz had thrown when making it rain. They really put on, and Vick was sure to have the DJ make special announcements all throughout the night about his cousin, street legend Parlay, who was about to come home from his long bid. Vick represented for his fam no doubt.

—

As with all beginnings in life, there is an ending. All life forms have an expiration date and a cycle that is to be no more. Melvin "Parlay" Anderson never fathomed the thought of being the one to pass off his wrong doings within the underworld to his dear mother. The sins of the son returned to claim the life of the woman who'd experienced the closest pain to death in order to bring him into this world. An elderly 73-year old woman was forced to pay the greatest penalty and suffer the ultimate sacrifice behind the ill-dealings of her son. She'd been beaten to a pulp by her attacker. The old woman was bludgeoned with a mini baseball bat, tortured, and then strangled to death. The nose, fingers, and ears of the old lady were snipped off. The brutal act was to send a clear message to the son—that he'd fucked up and angered the wrong person.

When the body was finally discovered, it was so badly eaten away, that all Melvin could do was plead with the mortician to do the best he could to make his mother suitable enough to be laid to rest in a better condition than she were. That was so because, before the killer departed the scene, he had specific orders to dump a plastic container of rotting fish guts, chicken skin, and maggot-infested liquid all over the body. He then was to open the cloth carry bag he carried, which had ten over-sized and hungry rats in it, and released them. Once turned loose, the rodents feasted on the corpse.

There weren't many in attendance at the graveside burial in the cemetery on 135th Street in Opalocka-Miami Florida, because Melvin decided on who would be present. For safety reasons obviously. Only about eight people were present in attendance.

As the reverend recited passages from the Bible, and the casket was being lowered, Melvin shed a tear, then another, and another. The rain cloud above finally weakened, and then its water broke, sending heavy drops to the earth and atop the fellow mourners paying their respects. Melvin had a visitor. An individual he'd never encountered before.

"Hey, Parlay," a voice called out to him. "Take a good look at the damage you've caused. What you have to say for yourself?"

"This ain't my fault. I had nothing to do with my mother being wrongfully killed. I didn't bring this upon her. Somebody made a terrible mistake. A *terrible* mistake!" Melvin replied in a vent of anger.

"So, how you figure, this was a *'terrible mistake,'* as you put it? From the way I see it, the sins of the son has come back to lay claim on the life of the mother, my dude. You have to reap what you've sown. No bad deed goes unpunished," capped the invisible spook.

"As I've said, I ain't have nothing to do with this. It ain't my fault!" Melvin fired back. "And why you seem to be attacking me with your words?" he felt the need to ask.

"Because, it's evident, nigga! It speaks for itself. Think about all the wrong shit you've done? The people you've shot? The people you've killed? All the dirt you got on your chest? The blood on your hands? The karma which shall stain your soul? Your day of reckoning is here and now, motherfucka'! There's enough room in that goddamn hole with your mammy for you too, my nigga!"

"Yo, what the fuck you say to me, my nigga?"

Melvin turned around to know who the voice belonged to. At the same time, a gun cocked. A loud horn blared. It appeared as if he looked "death" directly in the face, or so he thought, as there was no face on the hooded figure. There were only balls of fire in the sockets of the skull where the eyes belonged and nothing more. Also visible, was a set of rotting teeth, smiling at him. A humongous pistol raised and was situated one inch from Melvin's face.

"Now say one more word, nigga! I dare you!"

Melvin looked down the barrel of the firearm. All of his past bad deeds had played out on the big screen monitor right there before his very eyes. It was like a movie trailer in a sense, clips of multiple incidents. He held his mouth wide, as unfortunate fate leered at him. A blinding flash expelled from the gun. It was like an atom bomb had been detonated. Melvin began to shout at the top of his lungs, as blood spurted from his throat, spraying on others there by his side. Chaos ensued.

—

He jumped from his sleep in a cold sweat. Dude was still shouting as the fire alarm of the prison was going off.

"What the fuck! I better lay my ass off those K-2 strips and Xanax pills before I loose it for real! That shit a little too much for me," he scolded myself.

Suddenly, Parlay realized he'd been experiencing a nightmare. He spent the last night in prison inside of the isolation unit. A riot had broken out the same evening.

As the alarm continued to sound off, smoke blanketed the air. Dudes were flooding toilets and busting water sprinklers. It was complete disaster on all ends of the prison in those last hours of incarceration. *Complete disaster!*

Chapter 1

The Release Day For Melvin . . .

Parlay was the last passenger to exit the plane. His feet hit the turf of the hometown city as he slowly took in the South Florida air as a free man. Dude was glad to be back in the Sunshine to *"Gunshine"* state where he was born and raised. He held what little belongings there were to possess in a dark-colored tote bag, which was strapped to his shoulder. It definitely wasn't hard for people to detect that the guy had just been released from prison. He looked out of place, as his head roved in observance—in awe—of the modern technology and the updated fashion of the day. There wasn't too much about the surroundings he was familiar with anymore, since so much had changed in the seventeen years he'd been away.

There wasn't a need for him to retrieve anything from baggage claim, so he walked right past to the front lobby to await his ride. Parlay was draped in a pair of dark-blue True Religion jeans, a powder blue tee-shirt to match, a Miami Marlins fitted cap turned backwards, and a pair of Nike Air Jordan's Retro XI, the patent leather black and blue joints.

Along with the clothing, he'd also gotten blessed with a nice Citizen watch—an Eco-drive Pro Master Carbon. His lady Traci, had sent everything a few weeks before the release from FCI Fort Dix in New Jersey. He was out now, but would still have three years on supervised probation to complete.

Parlay walked over to the food section to get a bite to eat. Chick-fil-A was the place of choice. Throughout the prison bid, he'd seen enough of their commercials on TV to acquire a taste for the food. So, he was determined to have it as the first meal as a free man.

On his way back to the main lobby, he observed how everyone seemed so free-spirited. The people was much different than those he left behind—fat more calm, cool, and collected. It was an honor for him to be back among society and the diverse democracy there came to be. Never mind the fact that it seemed like people kept their eyes glued in on him, as if he looked on at them in an inordinate type of way. Or maybe he had. But it wasn't deliberate. It was the smell of freedom which had dude wanting to see it all. Or possibly, the looks was because they had an idea he was fresh out. Parlay was told that ex-cons have a certain type of aura about themselves other men in society don't, which made them magnets for women on the hunt for fresh meat.

Maybe that was what he was experiencing. Or *maybe* he was just paying more attention than he should've been.

Nonetheless, the people could've just been fascinated by the six-foot-four inch 226-pound black man, with the dark-brown complexion, and a healthy glow about himself. It wasn't like he was looking bad neither. Parlay was well put together with his low-cut Caesar style temp-fade, a five o'clock shadow of beard, and a pencil-thin mustache. The lineup was razor sharp.

There was this one particular light-skinned female in the area who really caught his eye. Actually, she'd been sweating him the whole time, and did everything imaginable to get his attention. Her body language that is. Like she wanted to be seen by him specifically. In all his years in the streets, it made it easy for him to discern that she was a 'working girl,' possibly, or at least that was what he thought. She was beautified in a major way—well-mannered, and wore Gucci and Christian Louboutin designer clothing. She was a stunning specimen of a woman. That bitch had it going on and was proportioned in all the right places.

She had a real professional disposition about herself, and looked like she'd got her grind on in whatever line of work she was into. Clearly, that was the one thing which hadn't changed much, in his opinion—ladies of the day, and freaks by the night. They were the ones out and about, chasing that almighty dollar, by indulging into the oldest profession in the world . . . *selling pussy.*

She stood in one area applying heavy coats of lip gloss and checking her appearance in the mini handheld mirror. Between tending to her looks, she winked at him a time or two. Parlay returned the gesture. The two flirted for a while before she invited herself over to where he stood. On the way towards him, his heart began to beat a notch above normal. Dude was experiencing a fit of anxiety.

Many years had passed since a woman took it upon themselves to step to him in this manner. And equally, many years had passed since he'd been *'chosen.'* He couldn't help but give her the attention she deserved. Shorty mandated that he do.

She finally reached his direct presence and was the first to speak. "Hello," she said. "How are you, sir? You're an attractive guy. Are you aware of that?" she asked.

Parlay was dumbfounded. Stuck on a shy note. He finally replied. "You not bad looking yourself. And I love the dress code you have."

"Well, I thank you," she said, as she caressed his shoulder. She gently stroked his toned arms. "You looking to have yourself a good time?" she asked another question.

"I don't know. Hell, I might be at some point or another in the near future. That is, if things don't go so well with me and my girlfriend."

"Oh! My apologies if you got the wrong impression. You can keep your girlfriend. I'm not looking to have a relationship. I'm only looking to tease and please you for a few hours—day or night—*if* you're into that type of action?"

"I'm a man, ain't I? What nigga you know ain't into *that* type of action? You and this bangin'-ass body of yours. You've been blessed. A nigga have to have lost all his brain cells to not acknowledge all of that you workin' with. I just got out of prison, as you—"

"I can tell," she cut in to say, smiling enticingly.

"But, umm, I gotta put your offer off for just a while, because I'm trying my best to do right by my girl."

"So you say, handsome fella. But you don't have *this lady right here* in your life," she said before brushing against him with her titties.

"But anyway, if you ever change your mind, please hit me up," she said and handed over a business card and a flyer from a gentlemen club. It read: *King of Dimez* (KOD). It had the name of the owner on it: *Raymond Eugene Stephens*.

Parlay held the business card in hand. "Thank you," he told her. He'd made a mental note of her name that was also printed on the card. "So, your name is, Yolanda C. Harris?" he asked.

"It is. But please, just call me by my stage name—'*Yola Sweets*.' It was a pleasure to meet you."

"It was my pleasure as well, Miss professional dancer. I'm Melvin Tyrell Anderson by the way, but everyone calls me by my street name, *Parlay.*"

"Okay, *Parlay*. I'll remember that. Don't forget, I sell dance moves, lap-dances, and leisure time. Not pussy or any other part of my body. You take care now, okay." she uttered before fast stepping out of the front doors, her Louis Vuitton luggage in tow.

The encounter with the dancer lasted about fifteen minutes. She was nice, and he'd already made up his mind to contact her in the near future. Yes, *indeed* he had.

Chapter 2

Traci, the girlfriend of Parlay, finally arrived to pick him up. He hadn't seen her in over six months, and there she stood right before him with no more visiting room restrictions. Now he was able to see her up close and personal.

Traci and Parlay had known each other for years before making things official. Even before his arrest. Prior to the relationship with his daughter's mother, he had known her for quite some time. She was actually his girlfriend at one point between the relationship with Belinda, his daughter Sherita's mother, and Chynesha, this female he was involved with at the time the cuffs got slapped on his wrists.

Although Traci had dealings with a few other dudes throughout the prison bid, when they reunited seven years ago while he was serving time, Traci vowed to stick it out with and not abandon him. She did, staying by the man's side through it all. And because she stuck it out, their relationship gained strength and durability.

Traci held him down and had even developed a bond with Parlay's mother and daughter. For that reason, he at least owed it to her, to give her his all—or at most the best part of him he had to offer—before becoming distracted and pursuing someone else. That distraction almost happened earlier there at the airport, when he met that pretty tender, Yolanda.

"Baby!" Traci shrieked, hopping out the car and running over to him.

14

Parlay wrapped his arms around her waist and pulled her in close. They tongued each other down right there on the spot, not giving a damn who saw them. After pulling apart, he tossed his bag into the backseat of Traci's new model Dodge Charger. He was proud of Traci. She'd really leveled up over the years in the medical field. After serving eight years in the Army, she pursued nursing and became registered at Jackson Memorial Hospital, eventually becoming an NP.

They'd both agreed not to let his mother know he would be getting out. Parlay wanted to surprise her. She had been under the impression he were to serve one more year. It was the story Traci and him fed to her. The two decided that after he'd gotten showered and dressed, that they would then go by his mother's and give her the surprise of her life. But first, there was business to get down between the two, because he was sure Traci's pussy was waiting for work to be put in on it.

Once they made it to her house, he quickly noticed how clean and well-organized Traci was. Parlay stood there admiring the place as she situated her car keys inside of a glass bowl that sat atop the coffee table in the living room.

"Melvin, please make yourself at home while I take a shower and get into something more comfortable," she said and smiled. "Something more to your liking."

"Okay, sweetie," he responded. "I'll do just that."

He sat his bag down on the floor next to a large China cabinet which covered the area. He then picked up the remote to the 80-inch big screen and turned the channel to **ESPN**.

While the television was playing, he went to investigate what was in the refrigerator. First thing dude did was pull open the produce drawer. Inside was varieties of fruit. He grabbed two bananas, a half bag of grapes, two ripened plums, and then fixed a tall glass of apple juice.

Having stopped by GNC on the way to Traci's, Parlay loaded up on a few things like, protein power, multi-vitamins, natural male enhancers, and gummy bear chews. He downed three vitamins, three enhancers, and the glass of apple juice. He wanted to ensure that he would be powered up and ready to beat the pussy down to the core once Traci got her ass out the shower.

In the meantime, Parlay gave God his thanks once more. He also went over in my mind every conversation Traci and him had ever discussed leading up to this day. He was truly hoping that everything would work out in their favor. Dude couldn't remember the last monogamous relationship that he'd had.

After a quick prayer and reflection, he left the television playing while taking a stroll through to see the rest of Traci's home. He wanted to see how she was really living. Upon entry of the master suite, which was one of four bedrooms in the house, he was stunned. The decor amazed him. Inside was a plush queen-sized bed with a canopy, dressers with huge circular mirrors, and specially decorated lamps that sat in separate corners. In Traci's closet, there was designer labels galore—Chanel, Gucci, Louis V, Fendi, Prada, and Hermes. All the shit that only celebrities could afford. The further he walked in, the more he took notice of the entire wardrobe Traci had. She'd even bought something for him as well. She had made sure he was taken good care of.

After finished admiring the closet, he headed back to the front of the house and into the dining room. There was high-end everything in there also.. There stood a Birch-wood and glass encasing which displayed fine silverware and dishes. Below was a mini wine cellar where she kept the best quality in champagne, vodka, and wine. She had it going on, and he was set to benefit from the quality of material and financial resources she held access to.

Chapter 3

Traci came out the shower with a black Victoria's Secret negligee on. Lord knows she was holding well in all the right places, with those proportioned assets of a lady who had maintained her quality. She applied Apple & Pear body lotion that had her skin glistening. The fragrance was amazing. Parlay caught a whiff of it as she made her way toward him. She sashayed and tossed those enticing hips from side to side. A grand display of femininity.

Traci had already worked him towards an erection. That wasn't hard to do. She stood directly in front of him, her legs parted wide, and her hands resting on her hips. He caught a glimpse of that puffy fat rabbit that seemed to smile at me from the furrow between those thick thighs.

"You think you ready for all this?" she sensually asked in a seductive tone.

Parlay palmed her ass cheeks and squeezed. "Hell yeah, I am. After all those years of being locked away, I better be."

"Ooh. Your touch is so pleasant, baby."

He smacked that thick juicy ass she had. "Is that right?"

"Absolutely," she purred.

"Well, let's get us something to blow on and relax first," he suggested.

As bad as dude wanted to get straight to the action, they didn't move too fast. As far as they was concerned, now that he was home, all the time in the world was at their disposal.

"That sounds good. You have a seat, and I'll cater to get us right," she stated, then disappearing.

Traci returned from the kitchen a short while later with two glasses and a bottle of pineapple *Ciroc*. She handed him a glass, then sat hers down while she went to the back of the house. Upon return, she had about an ounce of *Bubblegum Kush* in one hand, and a manual grinder in the other.

"Here baby," she said, handing him the contents in her hand.

She took a seat on the sofa beside Parlay, then crossed her legs. While he grind the bud and rolled it up in a grape-flavored *Cigarillo*, Traci sipped on her drink and watched. Once the weed was rolled, they blew two fat blunts—'hog legs'—and downed the Ciroc, then made their way to the bedroom—arm in arm, shoulder to shoulder.

First thing Parlay came out of when they got to the master suite was his pants, boxers, and wife-beater. Traci went to turn on the TV and put the sound on mute. She pulled out her iPhone and attached it to a mini speaker. Her playlist was a mixture of R&B, Hip Hop, jazz, and pop. Traci was a bona fide lover of music, so she had some of everything.

"I missed you so much, Melvin," she said, coming over towards him once more. "I'm glad you're finally home, baby."

"I missed you too, Traci. It's been a long time. A *very* long time."

"Well, you're here now, and the wait is over. We got the perfect opportunity to get off to a damn good start and do everything that we said we were going to do once you got released."

"So, how about we cut through the chase and get down to business, baby."

She smiled at the suggestion, and as they locked eyes, she straddled him. They stared deeply into each others souls, so to speak. Parlay took in all Traci's features—the cutest pointed nose, and beautiful eyes which sparkled white around the irises. She had an oval-shaped face and very well-set teeth. Her complexion reminded him of wild honey. She kept her hair stylish and impressive. She was beautiful—all five-foot-seven, 145-155 pounds of her.

Traci popped it off by caressing on Parlay's chest and shoulders. He returned the caresses on her amazing lady lumps, and traced along her 34-24-38 form. His hands explored everywhere. Her hands did the same. He could tell she appreciated the firmness of his chest, and the muscle definition he had. Years of hard work with the weights had gifted dude properly. His physique was on point.

After all the touching and teasing, he was charged-up and eager to get the show really going. The tongue-kissing ignited. It was so intense that he rolled her over and took command of the affair. It was several years of build-up he was determined to release.

Parlay nibbled on her titties before working his way down to her mid-section. He wasted no time putting his mouth on that fat rabbit situated between those slightly bow-legs of hers. Dude buried his face in her pussy and slurped delightfully while tickling the clit with the tip of his tongue. He then raised her legs to allow easy access to her pot of gold. He licked and slurped until he'd gotten her juices flowing. Her cup overflowed. He held a mouth full of her love potion. His intent was to *eat* it up before I *beat* it up . . . and nothing less than. It didn't take long to make her cream all over my lips.

After she'd came, he rose from his position so she could see the beast. In his mind, he was impossible to tame. Dude's manhood was already brick hard. It had been that way off and on since Traci had gotten her sexy ass out the shower.

"I like that," she purred as she sat up and positioned at the edge of the bed.

She then gripped his dick and popped it in her mouth real freaky-like. Because of the Altoid breath mints Traci had tossed in earlier, when she wrapped her mouth around his manhood, a tingling sensation shot through him.

"Whew!" he let out. She pulled on the meat-stick and bobbed a few times before she performed a deep throat, taking all nine inches.

With the tip of her tongue, she started at the very bottom of his sack, at the perineum, then she swiped upward past his testes, until she made it the tip of his dick head. Parlay damn near went into a full body spasm behind the sensational feeling he experienced. It was like I'd become paralyzed.

He released a light amount of pre-cum that he was sure ended up on her top lip. It didn't stop her though. She licked it off and didn't hesitate to swallow. When she stood to kiss him, he took her by the waist and eased her down onto the bed. We had no reason for protection because they both knew each other was clean. The proof was on paper and had been exchanged between them before he'd even got out.

Parlay hopped on top of her and slapped his manhood between the lips of her pussy, causing juices to splash all over her inner thighs. Her moans told him she loved the feeling it gave her. He eased his thick-veined shaft inside slowly, feeding her mini strokes along the way. Dude wanted to glaze every inch of my manhood with the froth of her cream. He allowed his girth to fill her as she panted, moaned, and called him out by name.

Traci attempted to back up, but she was unable to, because he had her pinned in place. He didn't want her running away. Only wanted her to feel all of what he had to offer. The plan wasn't to beat the pussy down, or to be too rough, so he slow the pace and flow.

The rhythm of his strokes seemed to match the beat of Bryson Tiller's *"Don't"* playing in the background. He eventually picked up the pace, then did a deep dive with each stroke. After a few minutes of good action in the missionary position, they switched it up to doggy-style. He wanted to hit the pussy from the back.

Parlay pulled Traci to the edge of the bed so she could get on all fours. He parted her ass-cheeks and began to eat the pussy again. The boy paid extra attention to her booty hole as well. She gyrated and pounced her backside in his face. His girl enjoyed the feeling. Since he wanted to stimulate her and pull the very freak from her soul, he continued giving her what she wanted, exactly how she loved it.

On sneak attack, he penetrated from the behind, and while doing so, thumbed her asshole sensuously at the same time. Gliding his manhood in and out of her love box had given him a top charge and gotten dude back to full throttle. Parlay began to work like no other in his efforts to get that first load off. It was the *real* re-entry to society for him.

While on lock down, just prior to release, he'd refrained from masturbation for a few weeks just for that particular occasion. So, the build-up was there, and he was ready to blow. For a moment, it seemed like he wasn't going to be able to climax. But then, he picked up the pace and really gave Traci the business. He humped so fast and so hard. Like a madman. At the same time, she threw it back at him. keeping the same energy. As his pelvic clashed into her ass-cheeks from the pounding, Traci creamed all over the dick heavily. The sound from the work he put in of his body clashing with hers, was like leather being slapped with a thin flat object. It popped like hell.

Traci's moans turned into a light scream. She'd fucked around and called him out by street name—*"Parlay."* That threw him for a loop, because she'd always—*always*—referred to him by his government name. He'd figured he must've been fucking her really good.

"Ooh, Parlay!" she screamed again. *"Damn!* This dick is so good baby. I love it."

At the point of her cumming, so did he. They came at the same time. The load he released was extra thick and gooey. Dude made a cream pie of her.

Hours later, Traci and Parlay got out of bed and hopped in the shower together. After they dressed, it was time to go and see Parlay's mother dearest. He was ready to see her too. But all of a sudden nervous to do so.

Chapter 4

On the way to his mother's house, he couldn't help but ask Traci to take the long route, so he could stroll through certain areas. Parlay wanted to see some of the streets he was familiar with, to see what remained the same, and what had changed, and in what ways. One of the places they'd passed was the Liberty Square Housing Projects, better known as the *"Pork-N-Bean."* For the last few years of his bid, he received many reports that the powers that be, had begun the process of knocking down the Bean. Also rumored to be torn down, was the Scott Projects and other popular hang outs or project communities. It was gentrification at it's best taking place. The whole agenda was to make sure that blacks ended up getting the worst end of it all. And that was the process going on.

Parlay's head roved aimlessly as he took in the many different faces. He didn't recognize any of them. Realistically speaking, the majority of dudes I had grown up with ended up in either one of two predicaments—dead or in prison. For the very few that had managed to avoid such fate, they'd turned out to be drug addicts, went broke, or were working low-paying jobs, struggling trying to make ends meet. They'd been reduced to literally nobodies. Not worthy of any honorable mention.

Parlay knew that there were some who wouldn't agree with a logic of his. But in a sense, prison saved him. It saved him from the perils and poison of street life. Prison had literally been a minute curse which brought him down only to lift him up again. He was just appreciative of the fact that he was still alive to tell his story. In the way he wanted it told.

After the purposeful long drive, they'd reached Parlay's mother's house. He had Traci knock on the door.

"Who is it?" his mother called out from inside.

"It's Traci, Mrs. Irene."

"Traci? You mean my boy Melvin's, Traci?"

"Yes ma'am. This me."

He had Traci do it this way so that his mother wouldn't get too excited prematurely. He didn't want her blood pressure to spike so much from the excitement.

His mother finally opened the door. "Hi, sweetie. What brings you here at this time of night? You normally call before you show up. What's the problem? Is something wrong? Lord Jesus, please don't tell me something's wrong with my boy?"

"No, no, Mrs. Irene. It ain't no problem at all. I'm here because of Melvin. But nothing bad has happened."

"Well, good. So, what about my Melvin?"

"It's the moment you been waiting for all these years, Mrs. Irene."

"Well, when do they plan to turn my boy loose? He's been in that God-forsaken place for far too long now."

"To tell you the truth, Mrs. Irene, he's already out," Traci stated.

"He is? That can't be so. Ain't no way in the devil, my boy got out of jail and not came by to see his momma. That can't be so, Traci. It can't. Where did you hear this from? And how did you hear it first, before the woman that brought him into the world?" she asked.

"I heard it from Melvin himself, Mrs. Irene. He got out today. And I was the one who picked him up from the airport."

"You did? Hot dog! The Lord knows he good. He is so good, I tell you. Well, where is he now?"

"He's out there in the car. Our plan was to surprise you. He wanted me to tell you first, because he didn't want you to have a fit from being too happy."

"Oh, that boy. The Lord finally answered my prayers and set my boy free. Tell him to bring his behind here, will you?"

Traci flashed the light from her cell phone as the signal. Parlay eased down the window and yelled. "Here I am, momma! I'm free at last!"

"Well come here, boy!" Mrs. Irene shouted excitedly.

He got out of the car and rushed into his mother's arms. Parlay loved his momma. She was the one person who knew him the best. The person whom still knew the innocence he had in him. The two hugged tightly with her holding onto him with all the strength she had. The only words Mrs. Irene kept repeating was, *My God is a mighty God. My God is a mighty-mighty God.*

An endless flow of tears streamed down the mother's face, soaking both their shirts. All the money in the world couldn't have gotten that shirt off of him. It would definitely be folded neatly, then situated in a vacuum-sealed bag, and stored away for sentimental purposes.

After he and his mother drew apart, Parlay took a step back to get an overall look at how well-preserved she was in her seventies. Although she'd visited a few times over the years, he hadn't quite seen her the way he was seeing her at that point. She was the true essence of a woman in terms of quality and virtue. Yes, it still belonged to her.

"Look at you, boy," she finally acknowledged, as she scanned her baby boy from top to bottom. "You look so good, son. Lord knows you do. No matter how old you get or what you may go through, you'll always be my baby, ya hear. Now I know I'm not the sharpest knife to cut fruit with, but, son, I know when a man has been with a woman," she said and smiled, then looked from me to Traci, and asked bluntly, "What you and Traci been doing all day?"

"Momma, you need to stop with all your mess. I ain't been with Traci. Although, in due time, I do want to give you another grand-baby. But I ain't been with Traci," he lied.

His mother turned to look at Traci so to gauge her body language and her energy. It was something that only other women knew to look for in each other. The two ladies in his life shared a smile that told its own story.

"Okay mister '*I ain't been with no woman.*' Boy, who you trying to fool. Remember one thing, son, you can *never* get one over on me. I went through the second pain to death to bring you into this world. And for two, I know the wiles and the ways of a woman."

Clearly, the mother was right. He couldn't get anything over on her. It was like she had an intuition from her soul when it came to him.

"Momma, you something else, you know that," he stated humorously.

The three smiled and shared a laugh together, then stepped into the living-room. In that instant, Parlay heard a voice call out from the back room. It was tender and pleasant.

"Mrs. Irene, is everything okay out there?"

Moments later, the owner of the voice appeared, in all her splendor and beauty. This woman stood at about five-foot-six, and probably weighed somewhere between 130 and 140 pounds. She wore nursing scrubs that fit superbly and tight. Parlay could tell by her figure that she worked out in her spare time. She was a natural beauty. He had already figured out that she was the nursing aide recently assigned to his mother's care. Dude was spellbound and captivated by her features. Even though he meant no disrespect to Traci, he was aware that she took notice of the extended gaze at the woman in the nurse uniform.

"Oh! Melvin," the mother said. "This is Porsche, my newest aide. I told you about her on the phone back when."

"Hello, Melvin!" Porsche exclaimed with a smile. She extended her hand for him to shake.

He gingerly cuffed her palm. "Your mother has told me so many amazing things about you. I've been with her for the past two months going strong. We've developed one of the most blessed bonds with each other. I couldn't have asked to be placed in a better situation."

"Is that right?" he responded, still holding onto her hand.

Traci had gotten tired of waiting to be acknowledged, and chimed in on her own accord. "And why is that, Miss Porsche?"

Parlay knew right then and there that Traci's tone was his direct order to turn Porsche's hand loose. And so, he did just that.

"Well, that's because Mrs. Irene shares a lot of her wisdom with me. They're priceless gems."

After the brief interaction between Parlay and Porsche, he looked at his mother for her response. He knew instantly that she felt the chemistry between the two. Long before his release from prison, the mother had been trying to put her matchmaking skills to use. From the moment Parlay held Porsche's hand, every detail of the conversations of the mother and son played over again in his mind. She'd always made sure to mention, *"her pretty new aide this . . . her pretty new aide that . . . ."* But *I thought momma liked and adored Traci?* he questioned. Actually she did, but that was probably up until the point when Porsche came along, and Mrs. Irene felt she would be a better match for her son.

"Momma, when was the last time you talked to Sherita?" Parlay asked.

"I spoke to her maybe a month ago. That girl doing real good for herself in college. She's making progress up there in Maryland."

Parlay's daughter was twenty-two years of age. Although he'd been gone from her life for seventeen of those years, they'd had numerous conversations. He was aware of many things she'd experienced—some pleasant, some not-so-pleasant. But they still held a solid bond and rapport with each other. In his baby's words, *"Daddy, you're the best male friend I've ever had."* He loved his baby-girl dearly.

"Oh yeah. Melvin, Rita and I have kept in touch as well," Traci said. "She texted me two weeks ago. She wanted to know if you were getting out on the date they had on BOP's website. I never told her the actual day that you were getting out, as you asked me to let us keep it a surprise."

Parlay smiled. "That's what's up."

"Actually, Melvin," Porsche interjected. "About three weeks ago, I was over visiting with Mrs. Irene, and Rita called. I let the two of them video chat on my iPad. You know Mrs. Irene don't know too much about all this technology available today. She mentioned something about coming home for spring break."

"Thank you for allowing my mother and daughter the chance to see one another while they talk. I'm sure that made my momma's day, to be able to see and talk to her one and only grandchild."

"Yes, baby, it sure was," the mother said to Porsche with a smile.

"Well, ladies." he caught everyone's attention. "I'm not trying to be rude or anything like that, but I really would love to get reacquainted with being home again."

It was already understood that he'd be staying with his mother for a few days before spending a full night at Traci's. Where the small issue came into play was when Traci became aware that *Porsche* would be staying over to assist his mother as her job required. He could see it in her face that she was uncomfortable with the thought of that. Traci had been golden to him when he was in prison. So he didn't have intentions on messing up what they had.

A few minutes later, Parlay walked Traci to her car. "You be sure to call me in the morning if you need a ride

RELENTLESS GOON | PRINCE A. TAUHID

somewhere. I don't go into work until four, so I'm free until then. Okay?"

"Okay, baby," he said, before giving her a sweet kiss. "I'll be sure to do that."

Parlay tongued her down once more before watching her pull off and head home. When Traci's car disappeared from the block, he went back inside to join his mother and Porsche.

"Baby, please don't pay my Melvin no mind," Mrs. Irene said to Porsche upon his return to their presence. "He's just a little shy, that's about it."

"What you talking about, momma?"

Porsche looked at him and they exchanged smiles. Little did she know, he'd been contemplating on how he would go about getting her interest. He wanted to get to know her in the best way possible. But right then, he was more interested in getting into the bedroom to see how it looked after all the years.

For the most part, everything was still intact the way he'd left it. He had to tilt his hat and salute the mother. She held everything down after the no-good father of his left them for a woman he'd met at church. Parlay didn't hate the man or anything like that. He just didn't fuck with him the way a son was truly supposed to fuck with their father. However, over the years while locked up, the two had come to reconcile their differences. Parlay's father had even made it his business to take a few trips to visit.

"Boy!" He heard his mother say, breaking the silence. "Come here and let momma see you again, won't you? Momma so happy you home. Look at how grown, tall, and handsome you've gotten." She grabbed his biceps and playfully squeezed. "You look strong too, son."

They stayed in the bedroom for a few minutes longer before heading back to the living-room to talk a little more. Once they sat down, the mother rubbed on his head and stroked gingerly about his face.

"Look at you, son. You so handsome. You going to make a good husband to a woman someday. I sure hope that day is soon. And look Melvin, why didn't you let me know you were getting out today? Had me thinking you were to do one more year." She released a joyous chuckle. "I could've made arrangements to come pick you up. Me and Porsche, here. Ain't that right Porsche, baby?"

"Momma, I told you that I wanted to surprise you."

"Son, now that you're free, what's your plans?" the mother asked.

"Yeah, Melvin," Porsche chimed in, "What do you plan to do for a living?"

"To tell y'all the truth, I can't really say at this particular time. I just want to enjoy being free for now. I've been blessed with a second chance at life, and that's my focus. But I do have to go and see those fuckin' crackas' Monday morning."

Parlay knew without a doubt that his black-ass had fucked up when he allowed his mother to hear him say the words that had come out of his mouth. He watched her immediately transform from a sweet, little, old lady, to a mad black woman. All in very short order.

"Boy!" she exclaimed. "Don't you *ever* let me hear you talk like that again in my house, you hear me! It wasn't those *crackas'* that took you off the streets for all those years. It wasn't those *crackas'* that prayed every night to keep you safe and healthy. So, don't ever let me hear you talk like that again, son. Ever!" she blasted.

He'd fucked up, and felt the need to correct himself. "I'm so sorry for that, momma. Please forgive me. And Porsche, I want to apologize to you as well, for having to see my momma out of character like this."

Porsche was the first to accept his apology, then the mother.

As the three of them continued talking into the night, at one point, Parlay noticed tears streak down his momma's face. He didn't understand why, but the more he thought about it, the more he'd figured that his mother was blaming herself for the poor choices and decisions he'd made in his own life. His mother was a southern woman in all her ways—strong-willed, family orientated, and God-fearing—and was deeply rooted in her religion. So, for him to have turned out the way that he did and made the terrible choices that he'd made, it probably caused her to feel as though she'd failed. But every man must take accountability for his own actions.

Mrs. Irene had told her son more times than he could remember that she was done on her end. That she had performed all she could as a mother and raised her boys. But it was him who'd chosen a different path than the one she'd carved out for them. He had given almost two decades of service to the system because he'd selected to be a gun and narcotics trafficker for a living. That was all on him. No one else.

Parlay accepted full responsibility for his shortcomings. He let his mother know that she did right by he and his elder brother, and that he was the one to mess things up. However, it seemed that it still stuck with her that she was the one to have failed.

Parlay dropped down to his knees in front of his mother as she cried.

"Momma, please don't cry. Please don't. I know and understand the hurt that you felt being here all alone for those years. And I'm sorry for that. I'll take the blame as I'm responsible for all you went through."

Guiding him up from the floor until he stood tall over her little frail body, she looked up at him directly in the eyes, and spoke her peace. "Prove yourself, son. Prove to me, to yourself, and before the presence of God, that right here at home, is where you truly want to be. That home and free, is where your heart lies."

31

There was a brief moment of silence. "Son, it's so easy to let the devil trick you back into that Godforsaken place. That's not what momma want for you. Your blessings and rewards are out here awaiting you to take advantage of them. All good things come to those that are patient and believe in the process."

He tilted so that his mother could plant a kiss on his forehead. After she left the room, he was alone to ponder over everything that they'd talked about.

Chapter 5

Parlay awoke the next morning feeling refreshed, energetic, and grateful to finally be free and resting well. Especially so since he was in the home that he was raised in. After his mother and himself shared that special moment with one another the night before, he and Porsche stayed up until around 11:30 having a conversation and getting acquainted. Traci did check in before he fell sound asleep, and he talked to her for about a half hour.

"Melvin, you plan to sleep all day? Or you going to get up and enjoy yourself of this meal that your momma prepared?" Mrs. Irene said to him.

His eyes opened as he regained focus. Drool oozed from his mouth, indicating that he'd rested well. He sat up on the edge of the bed with his feet planted firmly on the carpeted floor.

"I'll be there in a few minutes, momma."

Then and there, he gave the Creator praise and glory for allowing him the opportunity to see another day. Early in his prison sentence, there was an older guy whom he use to hang out with who'd taught him valuable lessons on life. The guy once said, *"Young blood, for as long as you live, always remember this much, if you don't remember nothing else I say to you. Be thankful and dutiful to God each and every day you wake up alive and healthy. Because there are many upon many, that didn't make it through the night. And as long as God made it possible for you to wake up and allowed you to let your feet hit the floor, then he has done his part. Everything else from that point is on you."*

Fifteen years later, those words still stuck with him.

Since Porsche's twelve-hour shift had ended at 6:00 a.m., it was just him and his mother for breakfast.

"And where might you be off to this morning, all dressed up and feeling yourself?" he asked his mother. "I thought we might be able to spend some quality time together today. You know, some mother-son type of time together."

"Well, son, if you *must* know, I'm going down the street today to Joanne's place to get my hair washed, pressed, and set for church Sunday. I left a spare key for you on the coffee table, son. Be sure to clean up good behind yourself, because Porsche works too hard for anyone to come along and make a bigger mess. And, son, please be sure to lock the door if you leave before I get back. Jewel will be here to pick me up in the next ten minutes."

He sat down to eat the breakfast his mother cooked. It was pancakes, beef sausage, cheese eggs, and grits. Throughout him eating, his mother popped back up in the kitchen to kiss him on the forehead before she left. "Son, I'm so glad you're home and out of that Godforsaken place. I truly am," she said, smiling in delight.

"I am too, momma."

A while later, once he'd taken a shower and gotten dressed, Parlay went on a walk through the hood. There was a lot of things that had changed. The old abandoned buildings or houses had either been knocked down or renovated. They were no longer an eye sore. New homes had also been built as well, and several businesses. The area seemed to be thriving. Along his stroll, he walked past the neighborhood corner store on 32nd Ave. he was familiar with. It had been there for years. Owned by Arabs now. There were a few dudes from the neighborhood posted outside the store. Much like the days of the past. He'd heard someone call him out by name.

"Say, that's you, Parlay? Is that you, my nigga? That can't be you, bro."

He stopped and slowly turned to find a familiar face. Only, he wasn't able to readily identify the person at first. But then, it came to him. It was a childhood friend of his, Fredrick Roberts. Dude had picked up about forty pounds, and was no longer the scrawny little nigga he used to be.

"Fred? Is that you in that big body now, my nigga? You done picked up some weight, playboy," Parlay joked.

"Yeah, it's me, but I don't go by that name no more, bruh. I go by *Four-Pound* now, homie. I'm a Blood. Murder-gang—sex, Money, Murder. Peter Rollock's Blood Set."

"You say what? When this happened?"

"Shit, maybe ten years ago when I went to prison. I been out going on three now. When them crackas' turned you loose, my nigga?"

"You won't believe this, bruh. But I got out yesterday. I only been free one day."

The two embraced, and then Fred stepped back to get a good look at his homie. "Damn, Parlay. You look like you been hard at work in the gym, dawg."

Parlay looked over all the diamonds and gold that Four-Pound had on. It didn't take a rocket scientist to figure out what he had going on.

"Trust me, bruh, I had to find a way to get that stress and frustration off my chest. Shit was not easy on my end making it through those hell holes I lived in. But I had to. And I'm here now. I see you been eating good out here too, home-boy," Parlay said to him.

With a slight chuckle, Four-Pound said, "Yeah, man. Life has been good for me since I got free. I'm making it out here for real, bruh."

He pulled a thick roll of money out his pocket. There was nothing but $100 and $50 bills that made up his knot. He peeled off ten $100 bills and handed them to Parlay.

35

"Here's a little something for now, my nigga. I know I don't owe you nothing, and I'm sure you probably racked up to the ceiling yourself. I just felt the need to do something any real nigga would do for a partner of theirs. Give me about three more weeks, and I'll really bless the game with more paper. Just keeping shit real with you," he said.

"I appreciate the love, bro," Parlay said, gladly accepting the gift. He put the money into his pocket. "You always been one of the real partners of mine. I thank you for those letters and whatnot when I was down too, my nigga. You kept shit real with me."

"Here," Four-Pound said. "Take my number and hit me up sometimes, bruh."

Parlay pulled out his cellphone and locked his number into the contacts. "I'll be sure to do that, bro."

"Maybe we can get some business up and going when the time is right," he said to Parlay.

"Yeah, bro. That sounds like a plan."

Moments after, a guy pulled up in a Tahoe truck looking to do business with Four-Pound. The S.U.V. he was pushing really caught Parlay's attention. It was solid black, and fully equipped. He'd always wanted to sit high and ride in something like that. Either the Tahoe or the Yukon Denali. Once he get his money right to do so when the leeway would allow, he definitely had plans to do just that. Buy himself one of the two.

They hugged once more before Parlay continued on about his way to the strip mall near where Flea Market USA used to be. It was good seeing his homie again, and he really appreciated the donation he made to his pockets. Parlay was for sure going to be reaching out to him to see about doing business at some point. Four-Pound could be really useful.

Chapter 6

Two Days Later . . .

Parlay and his cousin Vick, had plans to hangout the first Sunday of Parlay's freedom. They'd went to one of the most popular hood spots to socialize, a place called *The Tree* on 46th street NW. It was a little hole in the wall bar joint, that had a big-ass tree on the side of it. Sundays were the busiest days, and everybody that was somebody, would saturate the entire strip putting on and doing what they do. It would always be an all-day affair.

While there, Parlay came across a dude he thought was either dead or locked away in prison for a long time, because of the shit the guy had done in the streets throughout his past. His name was Ben, and he was a jack-boy. Dude loved to pull capers and do home invasions. His main targets was big dope-boys or dudes that were heavy in the game in other areas, such as weed and pills.

Parlay didn't know if or not Ben had done a prison bid while he was away, but he did know from others that Ben and some other partner in crime named Chip, tried to rob a guy for a kilo of cocaine and a set of twenty-eight-inch rims. In the process of the robbery, the intended target had managed to grab his AR-15 and fired away at the two. Ben was shot up and almost lost his life. The other cat Chip whom was with him, did get killed. Ben was blessed.

"Ben! What's good my nigga?" Parlay said to him while approaching.

Ben turned around. It took him a few seconds to do so, but he recognized who called him out by name. "Oh shit. Parlay. That's you? What up, fool? What's happenin'?"

"I'm good, nigga. What up with you? I heard about your problems while I was away."

"Yeah, man. I'm just out here trying to make it. I'm living and trying to get around to the best of my ability," he said, pointing to his cane and the prosthetic leg he now had. He then lifted his shirt to show the scars and wounds there. His entire mid-section looked like chopped liver. Ben was really fucked up.

"Shit, my nigga, the same life that I lived, turned out to be the same life to come back to do me harm. I can't do nothing but respect the game, you know. A nigga got to reap all the shit that they'd sown, homeboy," Ben started.

"Yeah, I'm sorry about that, man," responded Parlay.

"But how you been since you got out?" he inquired.

"I'm just trying to adjust to the free-world the best I can. From the looks of things, shit has gotten real crazy and desperate out here in these mean streets."

"Boy, has it! Shit crazy as a motherfucka,' my nigga. You just never know what the next day may turn out to be. One day, the money be plentiful and everybody eating, then the next, gas prices out the fucking roof, and we on the verge of another recession, with a terrible stock market."

"Yeah, man, I only hope that—"

Pop-Pop-Pop-Pop-Pop!
Pow-Pow-Pow!
Pop-Pop!
Pow . . . Pow!

Parlay's words were grounded out by the sudden eruption of gunshots. People began to scatter every which way in their efforts to get the fuck out of dodge. He and Ben both did the same and got the fuck on about their business before the police was to showed up. Vick had been inside the bar getting a few drinks at the time when the shots were fired.

Thankfully, he had parked far enough down the street to make it easy for them to get the hell on before other people and cars were all over the place, struggling trying to get out the area. Not long before Parlay reached Vick's car, Vick himself was running up behind him to unlock the doors. They jumped and hauled ass.

Vick peeled off in the Challenger Hell-Cat, burning rubber in the process. The way things played out with them driving off the way we had, it brought back memories of the night that Vick and Parlay went on a lick together and robbed a dude for three bricks of coke and $50,000. They'd fucked around and had to kill the nigga that night. The plan was only to break into the nigga's house, take what they'd went looking for, and get out of there. But shit didn't turn out as originally planned. Most often times it never does.

Parlay and Vick were related by their dads whom were brothers. And Vick was really like the brother Parlay never had, being that his actual elder brother, had been locked away in a mental-health asylum for many years, after someone slipped something into his drink at a bar he'd visited.

Parlay and Vick always hung out in the streets the most. Of all Parlay's so-called "friends" and street-niggaz whom claimed they fucked with him, Vick was one of very few to make it his business to send money, letters, and pictures throughout Parlay's entire bid. As mentioned, they'd always been close and never questioned the loyalty of the other. Vick may have looked after him the way he had while Parlay served time, because of the dirt they knew on one another. Especially the one related to an unsolved home-invasion which resulted in a murder that they was responsible for. Not saying that the two would ever rat on one another. But, it didn't matter who you were in relation to a nigga, you could never fully trust them, as they would never fully trust you.

—

On the night that Vick and Parlay went on the robbery mission when the murder occurred, they'd thoroughly checked the spot out long before they got itchy to go take what they knew dude held onto. They both had even dealt with Big Dre on many occasions, buying product from him to build trust and establish a rapport. They had done business with him many times to the point that he had welcomed them to his house in Carol-city. That was how they knew the spot so well.

The way they intended to set-up the robbery was, they'd called him to know if he was available. If he was, they had planned to just straight up rob the nigga. But if he wasn't, they were to simply break in his house and steal the contraband. Big Dre wasn't readily available.

The time was about 2:00 a.m. when they went to find out what the deal was. The two gained easy access into the house. They had no problem doing that. Once inside, they took a good look around and saw that Big Boy had upgraded since they last visited the place. Vick and Parlay ransacked and bombarded their way through the split-level two-story home in search of money and drugs. They came across four pistols in the process. A bonus, which Parlay had previously sold to him at the same house they'd now broken into. That was how they had a good idea that the money and the yayo were there, because that was how Big Dre paid him off, with drugs and cash.

As they scavenged through the basement laundry room, they came upon two assault rifles and the cocaine that they knew had to be stashed somewhere inside the place. Dre had the drugs wrapped very well in plastic and tape, situated in large bags of dog food stocked in the basement. He owned about eight game-breed pit-bulls as he had been active in the dog-fighting world as a heavyweight in the sport. The money was there in the home as well. It had been stashed in the *closet of the master bedroom, tucked away in $10,000 rolls inside a couple of suits that were in zip-up covers.*

"Jackpot!" was all all the words Parlay remembered Vick saying the moment he found the cash, as he was the one tearing the closet apart, and Parlay had been busy destroying other areas of the room.

As they prepared to leave, they saw Dre's truck pull up in the driveway, as Parlay peeped out the window to be sure the coast was clear before they exited the house. It wasn't.

"Just our luck, nigga! I thought you say he told you he would be out of town today?" Vick asked of Parlay through clenched teeth.

"That's what the nigga told me," Parlay replied. "I think he's by himself though, cuz. It's two of us and one of him. We can take that nigga down and tie his ass up if we have to," he added.

"Shit! We got to do something! You know damn well that that nigga ain't about to just let us walk out his house with his dope and money," Vick said as he pulled the P89 Ruger from his waistband and cocked it. Parlay then pulled his .44 Magnum from the ankle-strap he had on his left leg.

As quickly as they could, they put away everything they'd found and tied it up in a pillowcase. Vick ran over and stood guard at the door of the room to listen for Dre's footsteps if he was to come up the staircase. They both knew that there was a serious situation on their hands, since the only way out of the house was through the window into the backyard where the dogs were, and they would begin to bark, alerting Dre of intruders. The only other option was to go back down the stairs to be confronted by Big Dre, where he was sure to not go out bad without a fight.

All of a sudden, Big Dre was in the house and heading directly up the stairs, most likely towards the room that they were in. Parlay ran to hide out in the closet with his pistol still drawn, leaving Vick standing behind the door, prepared to ambush. Parlay peeked through the cracks of the door to observe the 6'7, 290 pound beast walk into the bedroom. He had a look of madness about his face at the sight of his house having been destroyed the way they had done to it. Parlay's heart began to beat extremely hard from the rush of adrenaline he was experiencing. Quite naturally, the first place that a person would run to take a look, would be where their money was put away at. And Parlay, was in the spot where the cash was, creating an inevitable confrontation.

He saw the beast turn and head towards where he was in the closet. Parlay hoped that Vick would react in time to knock the nigga out with one blow if possible. As Dre fast-stepped towards the closet, Vick ran up and busted that nigga on the back of the head with a second pistol he had on him Parlay knew nothing about. It was a .357 magnum and a heavy metal piece of weaponry. The blow only dazed Big Dre. And with Parlay knowing that the lick his cousin had put on dude was his signal to rush out of hiding and put a few hay-makers on him to assist in subduing the beast, he had to move fast. That turned out to be the exact course of action Parlay took. It only made matters worse.

Could you imagine the type of strength and fight that Big Dre put up against them? Vick would have fared better by simply shooting the nigga in the leg first, and then they would have had an easier time controlling the situation. But it didn't go that way. It went the other.

As the huge figure rushed at Parlay, all he heard was, "cuz, get out the way!"

A gunshot was fired.

Pow!

Vick popped that nigga in the upper left part of his back. The bullet must had pierced his heart, because the dead weight of the beast collapsed on top of Parlay like a pine tree freshly sawed to the ground. He was stuck underneath the body of a dead man. His eyes remained open as Parlay stared into them and saw nothing but death. He was able to maneuver from under him with the help of Vick. Once he got to his feet, he stood over Big Dre's body with his hands on top of his head and his mouth wide, in total shock and disbelief at it all. Years later, this particular incident would reappear to Parlay in a bad dream he would have, as he slept in his cell on the last day of doing the prison sentence he'd served.

"Come on, cuz! Let's get the fuck out of here!" Vick shouted.

They grabbed everything they'd found, ran down the stairs, out the door, and to the car located three blocks away. Parlay threw the pillowcase in the back seat along with the rifles and the pistols. Vick started the car and peeled off, burning rubber in the process.

The fast rubber burning get away had occurred twice while Vick and Parlay had been in the car together. And those, followed two separate shooting incidents that took place moments prior.

—

Twenty minutes after the shooting at *The Tree,* Parlay's phone vibrated. It was Traci calling. Apparently, the shooting victims had been taken to the hospital where she worked. It was located close by. One of the guys were DOA, and the other would survive. Although badly hurt, dude would make it. Being that Parlay mentioned to her that he was going to be hanging out at the spot—The Tree—she felt concerned and decided to check in on him. After he'd reassured her that he was fine, they ended the call.

Parlay then scrolled through the contacts of his phone and came across Yolanda's info. The two hadn't talked since she gave him her business card at the airport. Nonetheless, they did exchange a few text messages between the time.

Parlay texted while he and his cousin toured through the streets of Miami. Instead of replying by text, she called.

"Hello!" Parlay answered.

"Hey there, Melvin!" she responded in an excited fashion.

"Hey! How you been?" he asked her.

"I've been good. What about you?" Yolanda wanted to know.

"I've been good, sweetie. Just making sure to do everything necessary to stay out of trouble and remain a free man."

"I know that's the truth. So, you out and about, huh? What female has captured your attention since you been home?"

Parlay smiled to himself, knowing the question was a loaded one. Thinking she'd forgotten he'd told her he had a girlfriend already, he thought up a quick lie.

"I haven't had any dealings with no one. I've really been intent on being patient until the right one comes along. Who knows, you may be that particular one," Parlay stated in a matter of fact way.

"Okay-okay. So, tell me, Melvin. Have you made the call yet?" she asked.

"What? The call to you?"

She chuckled. "No, not me."

Puzzled, he questioned further, "What are you talking about? What call?"

"I take it that you didn't look inside your tote bag once you got home?"

"Nope. Tossed it to the side. It didn't have much in it besides my letters, my Bible, some photos, and legal material." He laughed it off. "Do I need to go back and look inside it?"

He heard a giggle escape her. "Go get what I left for you, and then call me back, say, tomorrow, or the day after, so we can discuss a few things. I would've mentioned it to you earlier, when we text, but I thought it would be better if I keep quiet and allow you to make the discovery yourself. Apparently, you didn't. So."

"Nah, I didn't. I'll definitely be sure to do so now. And yes, I can do that, but what is it I'm supposed to find in my bag?" he asked curiously.

"Ain't but one way to find out, right? Just be sure to keep in touch, and take care of yourself. I'll talk to you soon, hopefully."

"Alright. Later."

Shortly after the call, he received two text messages from Yolanda. One had a few links. The other had a few email addresses.

Parlay clicked on the one with the links first, and was immediately met with, *"Yola Sweetz,"* whom was Yolanda's alter ego. A slideshow of exotic pictures began to play. There were also several pictures of her at different photo-shoots with multiple themes in the background.

The second link directed him to a few video clips of her doing her thing on stage at a strip club. Yola Sweetz had a bangin' body for damn sure. She was out of this world sexy. And had just become even more appealing to him. He wanted to know more of her now.

—

"Yeah, Parlay," he heard his cousin say, snatching him out of the head space that he was in. "I got some real shit in the making, my nigga. Shit that's gon' help take me all the way over the top as soon as it's locked in. It's all about the connections with the people up top, and the foreign boys that got the import-export channels under control at the docks."

"That's what's up, cuz. The game plan was always to move up, right?"

"I know you always and forever a hustler, my nigga. It runs in our blood, cuz. We chest-deep in the game *and* the streets. So, of course, I know where your heart lies, P. Just let me know when you ready to get it poppin' again, and I'll quickly put you on board."

"I'll definitely do that, cuz. I just want to enjoy myself in the free-world first before I risk it all again. But aye, whatever happened to that pussy-ass nigga, Calvin? That bitch-ass nigga who gave sworn statements against me!"

"I don't know what came about of that nigga, cuz. After y'all went down, I ain't heard nothing else about him. How much time did he end up with anyway?" Vick asked.

"That faggot-ass nigga copped out for ten but only did eight," Parlay let him know.

"I tried my best to put it out on him, but had a hard time contacting cats on the inside to touch him for is. Karma is a bitch, though. And revenge is her specialty," Vick stated.

"Facts, cuz. Facts. But anyway, enough about that bitch-ass nigga. When the time comes, I'm in. I'll definitely let you know when I'm ready to jump back in the game."

"We really gone be big-time now, fam. Real talk. I'm making more paper now along the *'Iron-Pipeline'* than I ever have in my whole career in this gun-dealing shit. You see how I made sure you got right."

"Yeah, you did that, cuz. You took care of that."

"You motherfuckin' right, I did, my nigga. Family comes first."

As their conversation continued, the cousin laid out the details of the business for Parlay. So much had changed, as expected, but Parlay wanted to be sure that once he was ready to re-enter, Vick would coach him well and get things right.

After Vick dropped Parlay off at the house, Parlay was now eager to get to his tote bag. It was killing him to know what Yolanda had put in there. She had it sounding all cryptic and shit.

Upon entering, his mother was alone watching television. He greeted her and went straight to the bedroom for his bag. He unzipped it, and immediately saw an additional business card. It had a note attached:

Very nice job opportunity available as a security guard. Please contact Mitch and mention that Yolanda referred you.

Security guard? Parlay thought to himself. *What makes her think I'd be a good fit for that?*

His curiosity had gotten the best of him. And so, he dialed the number right away.

"Thank you for calling 'King of Dimez' Gentlemen Club, the most exotic haven on the planet. If you know your party's extension, please dial it at this time. If not, please hold. For Mr. Raymond, press one. For Mr. Mitchell, press two—"

He pressed "2," figuring that *Mitch* was short for Mitchell, according to Yolanda's words. His line rang three times before he answered.

"Mitch here. How may I help you?" some dude spoke in a South Florida cut with a Creole accented voice stated.

"Ah, yeah . . . Mitch. I was given a business card and told to contact you by a Yolanda."

"Yolanda, yeah . . . that's our girl. She must have referred you for the security position. Security is top priority to us. We need a bouncer or two. Yolanda must feel like you could fill that spot. But who am I speaking to?"

"I'm Melvin. But everyone calls me Parlay."

"Okay, I got you. Well, if all goes smoothly, and I bring you on board, we'll refer to you by Melvin, in more professional settings. We'll save the 'Parlay' for more leisure times."

"Okay. Okay."

"So have you heard of the club before you came into contact with Yolanda?"

"A time or two."

"A time or two!" Mitch retorted. "You must be from out of town or something, homie? Everybody knows about King of Dimez, playboy. We got 'em coming from all over to experience the culture here. We top quality."

"So y'all got it going on like that, huh?"

"You got that right!"

"I'll be honest, bro. I just recently got out the pen, after serving seventeen years. Been in the Feds and far away."

"Oh, okay. That explains everything," Mitch replied.

"You mind me asking how much is the pay?"

"Reasonable bro. Between two-fifty to a grand a night, depending. Plus, tips from the girls that's no less than twenty-five an hour from each one. If you interested, come on by Tuesday coming up at ten-thirty, and let us check you out. We'll go over everything from that point. Be sure to ask for me. If I'm not available, just come back when I am."

"Bet."

"Alright, I'm out. Stay up," Mitch concluded.

Parlay was intent on heading down to the club that upcoming Tuesday as suggested for the interview. He felt that being a bouncer and working at a strip club was something he could get used to.

Before his arrest, he knew all about the other strip joints of the Miami night life—CoCo's, Rolex, Baby Dolls, Club Ice, Black Gold, etc—but this new joint 'King of Dimez,' seemed to overshadow all its predecessors in class, celebrity allure, and finances. In other words, King of Dimez was the shit! It really had to have it going on, and Parlay was ready to get in where he was to fit in.

The world is mine! And all the dime-bitches that exist in it too! he thought to himself once the call was completed.

Chapter 7

Parlay took a long steamy shower in preparation for the interview and what could potentially be his first day on the job. He'd always been confident and optimistic so, foreseeing the best possible outcome was natural for him throughout any situation where there was a window of opportunity.

As he went through with his grooming ritual, the time was taken to express gratitude to the Most High, for allowing him his freedom restored. Dude expressed graciousness for being alive, for being healthy, and for being sane and able-bodied. He was thankful because, he knew there were a lot of others that didn't have the same blessings and who might probably never see freedom outside of prison walls again.

When it was all said and done, he stood before the full-length mirror, pleased at what stared back at me, and smiled at his reflection. The guy looked good. And marveled in admiration. Thanks to Traci, he was fitted in black Armani slacks, a black Armani button-down, a black vest, a Cordovan leather belt, and a pair of soft leather Italian wing tips shoes. He had on a pair of diamond-studded earrings with a pair of matching cuff-links. With a clean-shaven head and his beard superbly lined, Parlay was on point.

He dabbed his face, head, neck, and clothes with a portion of Muslim oil—the type better known as Burberry Sport—

and was now ready to roll. The intention was to make a bold statement with the way he presented himself.

Right on time, once he was done with everything, Vick hit his phone to let me know he was out front to pick him up. The ride to the club wouldn't take too long.

Once they arrived, Parlay hopped out in style and fly as ever.

"Thanks for picking me up and dropping me me off, fam," he said to Vick.

"No problem. You just be sure to get that job, so we can fuck most of those bitches up in there," he responded. "And not long before you got out, I had a party at the other spot in honor of you and my success in the game. Club Liv what I'm referring to. I wanted to have it here, but these niggaz demanded too much fuckin' money! It was a coming home party. One before you actually made it home. Just wanted to make niggaz aware that family was soon to rise again, and they better respect our hustle and grind out here," Vick stated.

"Oh yeah! But I'mma be sure to hook up with some bitches though, cuz. So be sure your dick still gets hard, alright," Parlay uttered then laughed at him before making his way to the front of the club.

—

Instantly, Parlay took notice of how long the line was. People were itching to get inside. The black guy whom controlled the front door was a huge figure of a man. Dude had to have twenty-four-inch arms or larger. He was at least six-foot-nine in height with the weight. He was tank-built, black, and as far as Parlay could tell, he took pride in flexing his authority. The bouncer doorman put Parlay in the mind of a dark-skinned Suge Knight. He was pumped up and jacked like a bodybuilder.

Parlay double checked himself as he got nearer.

"Not so fast, buddy!" The Goliath held out his hand in front of him. "Who the hell do you think you are? Only security, bartenders, dancers, and office people get an easy pass through my line. You can't just go straight in like you own the place. Now get to the back . All the way to the end of the line. And I'll see you again once your turn comes to pay here at the window."

Parlay tried to speak to make this man aware of whom he was and who he was there to see. But big boy wouldn't allow him a chance to get a word in. He just kept raging on. He'd generated a laugh or two with his slick comments, but Parlay wasn't all for the fun and games. Had he not been mature enough and placed value on his newfound freedom, dude probably would've unleashed the fire and fury which burned inside of him on the bouncer, and would have called that nigga out. Or simply took off on him by punching him in the mouth. But he was busy trying to be cool. No pressure on his end.

"Okay, so look," big boy continued. "If you don't have a V-I-P pass, one of the cards for that purpose, or if you ain't on this list here I hold in my hand, then guess what? You got to march your little happy go lucky ass, all the way to the back of this line here, like I've said, partner."

"You know what, big boy?" Parlay now stepped up to the challenge, preparing to level the humiliation caused upon him. "You really missed your calling, you know that? You should've been a body-building, muscle-bound, comedian, instead of a bouncer."

When the laughter from the line erupted, Parlay could tell that big boy didn't like being insulted himself. He could dish it, but, he for sure couldn't take it. Just as he inched a step closer to Parlay, trying to cause intimidation, Yolanda appeared out of nowhere.

"It's about time you made it, Melvin," she said. "Now, how is it gonna look for you to arrive late for your interview and potential first day?" she said, chewing him out.

"Am I late?" Truthfully, I did forget the time that Mitch had told me to stop by. But nonetheless, I'm here."

"Yeah, you late," Yolanda continued. "About forty-five minutes late, to be exact. No need to worry though, I covered for you with a good excuse of my own."

"Well, I definitely appreciate it. I also appreciate the potential opportunity."

Yolanda then grabbed Parlay by the hand and began escorting him through the door pass big boy.

"He's with me, and here to see Mitch," she announced.

Big boy mean-mugged before speaking. "Well, the next time, y'all be sure to let me know in advance, so I won't have some random stranger, attempting to breach my security. Okay."

"We understand, Bo," Yolanda stated, before we got going on our way.

As the two weaved through the crowd, they passed guys wearing bright neon lime green colored shirts with the words SECURITY SQUAD plastered across the front and back. Yolanda pointed and called out each person to him by name.

"That's *Cold World* right there. That's *Monsta.* He's *Riddick.* And there's more, but you'll meet them all in due time, if you get hired. The big fella that gave you a hard time at the front door, that's Bo Jack. He's cool. He doesn't mean any harm. Around here, security is taken very seriously. We have an A-list of patrons that come into the club, and the owners want them to feel safe at all times."

"Understood," Parlay replied.

As they continued towards the main office, Parlay was sure to compliment her in his own way. "You're too articulate and too professional to be a stripper," he said.

"Well, technically, Melvin, I'm *not* a stripper. I'm a professional dancer. I also have a business interest here at K.O.D. The term, *stripper*, is not one that I wear! It's cheap, and limited. And I do more than dance. I'm sure you didn't mean any harm. But, it's just that saying the word usually brings to mind, *bitch, hoe,* or *'hoochie!'* I'm none of those! And us girls, we make a lot of money. Sometimes more than drug dealers do."

Well, damn. She put me in my place, he thought

"Times have really changed, huh?" he said to her.

"They definitely have."

The two scaled the flight of stairs and reached the top tier. There was a VIP section, an exclusive bar, and a hallway which led to the door of the office that belonged to the owners. Once they'd reached the office door, they were immediately greeted by another member of security.

"Hey, Big Mix," Yolanda said. "This is Melvin. I'm bringing him to see Mitch and Ron. Mr. Raymond too, if he's here."

"Hey, Yolanda," Big Mix responded. He then threw his head back in a what's up gesture to greet Parlay before making a call on his walkie-talkie. "Yo, Ron!" he said into the device. "I got Yolanda and the new guy, Melvin, here at the door."

"Okay. Bring them in," Ron replied.

After Big Mix let them into the lounge area of the office, he returned to his post. Parlay was in awe at all he took notice of beyond the two heavily-tinted doors. The whole time he was thinking to himself, *Whoever these cats is that owns the spot, has his empire all the way together.*

Yolanda and Parlay stood in place waiting for Ron to walk through the door. In the meantime, Parlay continued to admire the twenty-by-eight foot fish tank that was built into the wall. The whole thing was damn near a wall itself. Inside the tank, there had to be somewhere around forty tropical fish. They gracefully swam about on the inside of the lavish glass casing. Not only that, but the damn tank had a foot long shark patrolling the waters as well. That shit was so off the chain for Parlay to witness.

These Dudes for real got it going on, he *further* thought.

Soon, Ron appeared. But he wasn't alone. There was a shorter guy alongside him, wearing a gray suit.

"Melvin, this is Mitch," Yolanda introduced. "Mitch, this is Melvin."

"*Oh*, this Mitch," he let out. "The guy I spoke with on the phone." Parlay extended his hand to shake Mitch's. "It's a pleasure to meet you, sir."

"Likewise, my guy. So, Yolanda here tells us that you'd be a good fit for our security team."

Parlay looked from Yolanda to the two gentlemen. "I believe that I would be. I can tell that you take care of your employees. And I can for sure see how you handle business."

"Good observation. Yolanda might know something about recruiting talent," Mitch said, as he looked over to observe her smiling. "And I'm sure she's made you aware that she has an invested interest in the company as well. She's got management rights in the branding and entertainment department of *King of Dimez.*"

Parlay nodded. "Yeah, she's made me aware."

"Good. I said all that to say this. With her recommending you, that holds weight in our view. It also means, that certain aspects of the job will require you to report directly to her. In matters of security, you'd report to the Chief of Security. Chief of Security is the one through the door right there."

"Big Mix right?" Parlay stated.

"Right. Big Mix. Now, another thing, Melvin." His expression went blank. "Do you think it's possible for you to work here at *King of Dimez* around all this temptation, and still remain level-headed enough to function properly?"

"That's definitely possible, Mr. Collins."

"Please, just call me Mitch. Yolanda has spoken so highly of you. The only thing left was to just meet you in person, talk to you face-to-face like two men are supposed to, and proceed from that point."

"It's a great honor, especially for me. Coming from where I come. I look forward to doing nothing but the absolute best, in work *and* in my commitment to loyalty."

"Good! Because that's exactly what we need here at club K.O.D., an additional motherfucka' who knows a thing or two about loyalty and priorities. You couldn't have put it better," Mitch stated emphatically in his South Florida cut with Haitian-creole drawl. It matched the one tone heard when the two first talked on the phone.

"I'm ready for y'all, Mitch."

There was a voice which came through over his walkie-talkie.

"Bet that," Mitch replied. He turned to Parlay and Yolanda. "Mr. Raymond is ready for us," he announced. "You guys follow me," he said, heading back in the direction he'd previously exited.

Chapter 8

A short moment later, they all entered Mr. Raymond's office. Parlay wasn't expecting him to be present, but he was. He looked as if he belonged to the Watutsi tribe in the African Country of Rwanda. He had a nose that resembled a bird's beak, and his complexion reminded Parlay of freight train oil. Black as the darkest of night. He was tall. Stood almost seven feet, easily towering over the desk he stood behind. Dude had on a grey designer pinstriped suit. That thing cost every bit of $3,000. Parlay knew this because he'd saw one similar in an issue of the *Robb Report* magazine. Looking at him put Parlay in the mind of the great NBA legend, Ralph Sampson. He was clean-shaven in the same way, well-groomed, and even wore his hair in a similar fashion.

Immediately, Parlay noticed a stack of money sitting atop a silver briefcase. Along with the money, was also paperwork, and a chrome .45 with a pearl handle.

Mr. Raymond, bypassed any greetings and cut straight through the chase. "So, you feel as though you're fit to start tonight, Melvin?"

"I feel I may be, *if* I get the job," he quickly replied.

He nodded slowly. "By the way, I'm *RES*. It's the first letters of my full name: *Raymond Eugene Stephens*. But for now, you can call me, Mr. Raymond." He extended his hand to shake his guest's.

"From the looks of things, you're on your way to being on team K.O.D. Yolanda referred you. And Mitch has already given me the nod of approval. Not to mention you made it to my office for me to finalize it all. Congratulations, son! You're hired! We'll put you down as temporary for now, but eventually, you'll transition to full time. I get a good vibe off your energy." He sized up Parlay long before concluding with the following words. "I believe you'll turn out to be a good one," he said.

"I thank you for the chance you've given me, sir." Parlay turned to look at Mitch and Yolanda who were both nearby. "Thank you to all of you that played a part in me getting hired. I promise not to let you down."

"Okay, cool," Mr. Raymond said. "Now, I need for you to fill out this contract here. Be sure to carefully read everything. Okay, son? I got to cover my own ass to prevent any potential lawsuits. Yolanda here will assist you through it all. And once you're done, you'll be officially part of the team. I'm serious about loyalty. I'm also big on commitment and professionalism. You understand?"

"Yes, sir. I clearly understand."

"Once again congratulations and welcome aboard!"

A short while later, Parlay completed filling out the contract and was in one of the neon shirts that he saw on the other guys upon first entering the club. Before long, it was just he and Big Mix, whom had immediately begun lecturing him on the rules and regulations. Mix did a few demonstrations for hypothetical scenarios, as well as showed the new protege all the fire routes, and all things safety for the club.

"Check this out, Melvin. I'm going to give it to you straight with no cut on it, alright. Our main job, is to make sure, don't a fucking thing happen to our girls! Period! Because if it wasn't for them, there would be no *King of Dimez!* Also, we got to be sure that these crazy-ass dudes don't come through here shooting and tearing up the place.

Basically, we protect, and preserve the integrity of the club—and its owners.

"I follow," Parlay confirmed.

He really respected the way that Big Mix articulated himself. Sadly though, he had always thought that big, black, bald-headed, swollen muscle bound niggaz, had little to zero intelligence. Basically all muscle and no damn brain. Big Mix really had him fooled.

Big Mix pulled two laminated post cards from his pocket. They were the size of the ones that people played poker with. On them were different codes that were to be used over the radio.

"Here," he said. "It belongs to you. Be sure to learn this shit in fast order," he dictated. "Like you had to learn your prayers, or your grace before you was allowed to eat."

"I'll do that for sure. And as far as guarding the girls, I know that there's some sick lunatic stalkers out there in this crazy chaotic world we live in. But I promise you, these girls will be safe on my watch. I just got out of prison after doing damn near two decades in that bitch, and Mr. Raymond provided me with the opportunity of a lifetime. I value and respect that shit to the fullest. I ain't even been out a full week yet, and here it is. I got a job working at one of the hottest clubs in the country. I'm giving it my all, bro. You feel me!"

Big Mix nodded in approval and smiled. "That's what's up," he said.

Chapter 9

Big Mix called for another guy to take Parlay on a tour of the club. There were a lot of introductions that had to be made. He then directed for him to go meet up and have a word with Tisha, the head bartender. Tisha was also Mitch's daughter.

He approached the spacious well-equipped bar in search of Tisha.

"Hey! I was told to come find Tisha over here," he said to the woman behind the bar.

Seeing that he was the new jack on the block, she eye-balled him from top to bottom, taking in all of his personal stock. She pointed in a direction. "Tisha would be that girl right there with the short sassy hair-do. But, if she can't help you with what you looking for, I won't be too hard to find." She was a coat of brown sugar, thick, and had a seductive figure. "I'm Freda," she said. "What's your name?"

"It's Melvin, but please, call me Parlay."

"New guy, huh? Okay, Parlay. It's nice to meet you."

"It's nice to meet you too, Freda."

"Well, I'll be seeing you around . . . *Parlay*."

"Indeed. Indeed you will."

Once he'd reached the end of the bar where Ms. Tisha was, he became intoxicated by the cuteness of the ebony sensation. As she graced him with those illuminating and compelling eyes of hers, she spoke. "So, what will it be for you, sir?"

"I was told that I should speak with you. I'm the new guy on security. Big Mix sent me your way."

"Is that so, new guy that's a part of the security team."

"That's correct."

"Well, the main reason Mix told you to come and speak with me is because, there will be times where it will be a rotation of you guys to escort me upstairs to the main money room. I have to go up there to drop off large amounts of cash. Some nights, I have to make two to three trips. I may utilize the same guy each time, or I may alternate. depending."

After Tisha filled Parlay in on the order of rotation, she took him to meet each of the drink mixers who were supervised and had to report to her. After introductions were over, the two chatted for a while. His mind kept going towards her beauty. She was rocking the hell out of that sassy short hair-do. He liked it. Her eye contact and energy was incredible. She had true power in her spirit to magnetically draw and attract. It scared Parlay in a sense. At no time had he'd been compelled by the presence of a female in that way in almost twenty years. It was hypnotic.

He wanted to keep the conversation going, so the natural thing to do was to continue talking. The whole time, he'd hoped that he wouldn't be called upon to rescue anybody.

"From the looks of things, it's pretty peaceful up in here," he declared in observance.

"Yeah, it's a pleasant energy, for the most part. But let's hope it stays this way."

"Okay, well, don't be afraid to call if need be."

She laughed a little. "Trust me, I won't. It goes with the job."

When they were done talking, Parlay went in search of Big Mix. Back in his presence, he mentioned Tisha to him, for elaboration.

"Yo, Mix, Tisha a piece of work, huh."

Mix cracked a smile to reveal six gold teeth at the top row of his mouth. "You think so?"

"Well, she didn't come off as a snob or anything like that. Actually, I got a damn good vibe from her. She has a nice sense of humor. But at the same time, I can tell she can be serious too. When she was explaining things to me, she wanted me to focus and give full attention to what she was saying."

"Yeah, that's definitely Tisha, my brother. She's put together. I directed you to go and have a word with her to establish a decent rapport."

"It was a nice conversation. Lot of respect for how she handles herself," Parlay admitted.

"About a year ago, we had this crazy-ass nigga come up through here on some high shit, and drunk out of his fucking mind! The clown must have been wigging out on ICE or something. He goes to the bar where Tisha's at, orders a few drinks, pays for them with five, ten-dollar bills. He mistakenly *thought* he'd given the bartender five *$100* bills. He began demanding his money back from the young lady that rang his tab. Dude gets into a fussing fit about his change not being given to him, and then starts to curse the girl out. Tisha approaches to address the situation without security. She explains that he made a mistake, because club policy is, everyone that has bills over twenty dollars, must exchange them out at the money window to prevent any counterfeit currency from circulating. Anyway, dude continues accusing the girl of trying to steal his money. Then, he fucked up and spit in Tisha's face. What the fuck he do that for! Tisha tossed a drink on him and then reached for the whistle around her neck to alert us. Before we could get there, dude grabbed Tisha around the throat and began to viciously assault her. He broke her nose and knocked out four of her top teeth. We beat that nigga senseless! We damn near killed that nigga! Hell, Mitch probably *did* have that nigga wiped out, putting his hands his daughter. He paid top dollar to have Tisha's nose and teeth fixed. The best doctor and dentist money could pay for took care of her. I mean he kicked out a grip too. Like $100,000," Mix made Parlay aware.

Suddenly, Parlay's attention was captured by the DJ.

"And now, I want y'all to show some love for two of the baddest dancers that K.O.D. has to offer. It's Pocahontas and Luscious Lola," he announced.

The crowd went crazy.

Pocahontas appeared with two long braids, looking like she was either Native American or Mexican. A hot piece of ass though. And Miss Luscious Lola, that white bitch was a thick amazon by all means. She had on a cowgirl hat, and a mask to complement the outfit. Also, she was wearing a vest to hold up those nice titties she had, as those water balloons jumped and jiggled—to the left and to the right, then up and down.

As far as the dance routine, they were comfortable with each other and played off the rhythm and flow the opposite gave off. It was evident they'd possibly participated in the acts of licking clits and bumping pussy prior to. Maybe so. Maybe not. It certainly appeared that way.

Once the set ended for the duo, a few of the other girls came out to perform. Boy, did those tender dick having niggaz throw all of their money away.

Parlay peeped at my watch and saw it was still early, only 11:49 p.m. He paced around the club on patrol looking for any abnormal activity. He spotted Yolanda in a conversation with a guy. The look on her face and her body language seemed off. His discernment was that dude may have been drunk or something to the effort of. As a precaution, Parlay approached. Right as he did so, the guy tried to put his hands between Yolanda's legs to grope her.

"Hey, watch that!" she shouted. "What is wrong with you! Get a hold of yourself, dude."

Parlay was needed to intervene. "Yo, buddy! How many times she got to tell you to stop touching her?" he ranted.

The guy then grabbed her by both arms. Parlay knocked his hands down as he got up in his face.

"If you got a problem keeping your hands to yourself, then find someplace else to get your rocks off, because it won't be here!"

The moment he staggered towards Parlay was when he knew shit was about to get real. With incoherent speech, dude yelled, "Nigga! Who the fuck you supposed to be! Captain Save a Hoe, or something! Fuck-nigga!"

"Melvin. This guy is completely obsessed with me. He thinks because he has thrown plenty of money my way, that I'm required to give him extra attention. Not only that, this nasty bastard tried to grab my ass and feel on my private. Nigga better go find a cheap trick for that shit! I ain't the one!"

"Bitch—" he attempted to say.

But right then, anything he had to say, was cut off when Parlay reached for him. He tried to choke the life out of buddy. Before long, it wasn't just Parlay by himself. There were four more bouncers present to assist. Together, the five of them lifted that nigga in the air and headed to the door with him. Once they'd made it to the outside, they tossed his ass to the pavement.

"Nigga, don't ever come back, until you got some manners and can show some respect!" Parlay spat.

Chapter 10

Two Weeks Later . . .

Parlay was back on the job for the third week in a row. He found a great love and joy for the employment opportunity he'd been afforded by Mr. Raymond. Yolanda had really put him in good standing with the boss and the co-owner. She had to have seen something in dude that really inspired and motivated her to approach the way she did at the airport that day. To the date, she still had not revealed to him what it was that she adored about him to caused her to get him the job, nor what was observed of his character which compelled her to introduce herself in the way she had. The two had yet to have an in-depth conversation to truly discuss the likes and other attributes which they admired in the other. Parlay held high thoughts and regards for her in many ways.

For some strange reason, he discovered a different take and perspective of her, being that he knew she held her own and kept shit real by all means. But he couldn't quite figure out exactly what her over all ambition or objective seemed to be. He was puzzled by the way she moved, conducted and carried herself, and how she handled her business. Dude really desired to know the full involvement and interest she had in K.O.D.

Why would she continue to dance as a stripper at the club if she didn't have to? he questioned himself. She began to become a mystery of some sort. Perplexing, as no other.

On that particular weekend, K.O.D. had big ballers and breadwinners to show up and toss their cash so to experience the atmosphere of the club had to offer. Yolanda decided to work as a dancer this Saturday night, but was only to perform on the stage a brief moment. She and Parlay had occasionally locked eyes and exchanged smiles as they crossed each others path throughout certain points of the night. He went about with his duties and made rounds to check and see that the other girls were okay. Along the stroll, he was stopped by one of his bouncer co-workers.

"Say, Mel. Mr. Raymond wants to have a word with you, bro," the guy said.

"Oh, yeah," Parlay replied.

"Yeah. He up in the VIP in his special little section at the bar."

The both of them headed his way. Mr. Raymond found himself busy chopping it up with this other guy whom had on a very exquisite and expensive silver pinstriped suit and a pair of top dollar alligator shoes on his feet. Parlay had no knowledge what lifestyle the guy lived, but, the guy he encountered talking with Mr. Raymond, fit the appearance and characteristics of being in the running for top pimp in the country. He dabbed and finessed his limbs in animation as you would see those actual Mack-Men putting on.

"Look, player, I don't give a damn what the cost gonna be. You just make it happen as soon as you can, home-boy. Don't you know that these motherfuckas' will be busy trying to break down the door to get up in this bitch, if I had *Cardi B* performing, along with the best girls in the stripping business getting loose in the building!" the boss Mr. Raymond excitedly proclaimed.

"I'll see what we can do," Mr. GQ replied.

Mr. Raymond observed Parlay had answered to his summons and made one last remark to his company before his attention went towards the new employee.

"Yeah, my brother. You do that, will you. Make it happen," Mr. Raymond stated to the man. "So, how things been going for you, Melvin?" he asked.

"Everything good, Mr. Raymond. *Life* is good, you know," Parlay replied.

Mr. Raymond, the strip club king, fired up a cigar and then leaned back on the sofa and cross his legs. It was as if he personified the black business-man Reginald Lewis, who wrote the book, *Why Should White Guys Have All the Fun.*

"I been meaning to say something to you. I like how you handled that situation a couple weeks ago for Yolanda. I was impressed, I must say," he stated.

In a confident manner, Parlay replied, "At times, a few problems can be defused and resolved without getting too physical, if you know what I mean. Besides, I'm not trying to make an enemy with no one. I only seek to align myself with those that call shots and make things happen in a powerful way."

He took a seat across from Mr. Raymond and leaned in to continue with the talk they were having. Mr. Raymond leaned in and patted the young man on the shoulder along with smile at him. "You're going to work out just fine, I do believe. Just fine, my guy," he said.

With no further words, Mr. Raymond stood to his feet to dab himself and prepared to step off. He left a trail of tobacco smoke in his path as he and his company departed. As always, Big Mix was his escort, and as big and wide as his body was, he was like a huge collage that covered everything about Mr. Raymond in physicality.

At the sight of the size Big Mix was from Parlay's viewpoint, it brought back to memory a "larger than life" physical feature of another "big man" he'd encountered at one point in his years of living. The Federal judge whom imposed the 240 month sentence on him in the district court there in Miami. Dude himself had a bit of girth on his short and overtly stout body. A fat man. Built like the character the Penguin on Batman.

That bastard seemed to be determined and eager as ever to send away Parlay's young, black, and troubled ass for a long time. Once he rendered his ruling, at the acceptance of the guilty-plea agreement, the only voice which was heard from that moment forward was that of his mother, *"Oh God! No, your honor! Please! Lord Jesus, no! He's just a boy! He's too young for that much time!"*

Parlay happened to turn in the direction where his mother was standing to get a good look at her. He saw a few others whom assisted in holding her up on her feet to prevent from collapsing to the floor out of distress. A strong sense of embarrassment had overtaken him. He'd disgraced his family. And most of all, he'd violated each and every valuable lesson his mother had taught him regarding staying out of trouble and not placing himself in any predicament that she wouldn't be able to help him get out of. Long story short, Parlay was shitted on by the co-defendant he had, a Calvin Prescott.

—

For the first five years that Parlay was locked up, he'd vowed to seek revenge and make that nigga CP suffer for his acts of betrayal. There had been so much rage built up inside him, to the point that he'd developed a bitter attitude toward many people. Dude stayed getting into fights, until the day he befriended this old-school guy whom helped him get his priorities together by sitting him down and having a heart-to-heart with the young buck on relevant matters of life. Parlay seemed to have learned a lot from that wise brother. But was he willing to let it show in his actions? This became the question.

Once more, Parlay had been brought back to reality by the sheer grace and opulence of Yolanda's beauty.

"Let me mess around and find out one of these club hotties have gotten the best of you, and now you can't keep them off your mind," Yolanda said with a smile and a laugh.

"Nah. It's nothing like that, my girl. I was just trying to figure out ways to elevate to the point where I can get some real money to put down on a club. A nice ride too. That would do me just fine. Mr. Raymond has really inspired me in a major way. I like his style and respect the way he handles his business," he stated in an assertive way.

"Well, I don't know about the club part. But why haven't you said something about a ride beforehand, silly? I passed by a spot that had a nice Chevy Tahoe for sell. It was in mint condition. I test drove it and all. I was contemplating buying it for myself but decided I would rather have a car instead. The Tahoe only got 5,000 miles on it. I think that will be the perfect vehicle for you," she said to Parlay.

"I wouldn't mind checking it out if you got the time to take me? I got to go and get my license reinstated first though."

"Yeah, get your license situated first. In the meantime, we could still go by for you to take a look," Yolanda suggested.

"Yeah, we can do that. I'll have the money withdrawn and give you a call."

"That sounds great," she lastly stated on that subject.

"Also, Yolanda." he got her attention once more. "I'm trying to figure out why we haven't engaged in a deep conversation yet."

"In due time, dear, we will. I can promise you on that. In due time," she assured and left him with that much.

He could tell that something was up with her, because she appeared a little too excited.

"Well, excuse me for a moment, if you will. I have some other business to attend to," she said.

"No problem, Ms. lady. Go right on ahead," he replied, refocusing on his post he manned.

The girls had been slated to make anywhere from $10,000 to $20,000 each that weekend as it turned out to be a big celebrity showing at the club. Some held potential to make more, depending on how well they put in their work.

Parlay scanned the club seeking to detect any aggressive tension or disturbances. None were observed. Big Mix was located in a secluded corner in VIP deep in conversation with one of the girls. Parlay approached in a nonchalant way to greet the two.

"Pardon me, Mix. Everything looks good on my end. Nothing out the ordinary," he informed.

"That's what's up, bro," Mix responded.

"Do I need to continue holding things down on this end or return to ground level?" Parlay next inquired

"You good up here for the time being. No need to oversee. I'm about to take this area. I was on break."

"So, you good?" Parlay asked.

"Yeah, I'm good," Mix answered.

Dude got the impression that he may had interrupted something private between Mix and the female, or something even more serious of nature. But being that Mix was his supervisor, he had to check with him on the strength of being relieved from the particular post he looked over. At his approach, the demeanor of Mix and the chick had drastically changed. It was as if they'd silently told on themselves about something.

"Yeah, bro, everything good. I'm just here letting my people know the time I get off tonight, so she can hook me up with her home-girl. That's about it," Mix said as he looked up at Parlay along with the female who accompanied him.

Mix could have been nominated for best actor award with his performance. The crazy part about it was that, he had assumed Parlay didn't recognize he'd been ducked off in the dark corner for the length of time he had with one of the dancers of the club. Parlay saw him the moment he had taken a seat. The club had a policy that restricted security from

69

interacting and getting too close and personal with the girls, so to not compromise or breach security. But Parlay figured, who was he, to mention any of that to Big Mix?

He was more than sure Mix had such leeway to do as he saw fit, with the nod from Mr. Raymond. And Parlay had no intention of speaking on anything. His mother had always reminded him of the famous cliché, *"For all things in the dark, they will soon be brought to the light."*

Following a quick round and security check, Parlay propped himself up against the railing on the second level opposite VIP. He was overlooking the bottom floor, when suddenly, the lights went dim. The only time that such moment occurred was when a very exotic and appealing dancer was set to perform on the stage. The DJ made an announcement.

"Alright, y'all. Let's turn the motherfuckin' temperature up for sho' for the next dancer, as she entices your mind and tickle your desires with her mystery. Give it up, for the sensational, Yola Sweetz!"

Yola Sweetz? Parlay thought. That was Yolanda's stage name.

As the track began to play, everyone's attention was placed on the curtain as they all waited for it to open. The limelight heightened the sense of curiosity and anxiousness in the atmosphere. Suddenly, appearing wearing a partial tux, a top hat and strutting with a cane that had a gold-plated cobra as the handle to complement the outfit, the lady of the hour, made her presence known. With the hat tilted to the side, it gave her a bossy-sassy type of look, as she dapper and stepped along with the beat and dropped to the floor in back to back splits like she had no joints. She slowly eased up and snaked her body across the floor, creating an ambiance as she maneuvered. It was like she was making love to an invisible man beneath her.

As Yola Sweetz got to her feet to perform other aspects of her set, she tossed the cane and the hat to the side. And then, she seductively removed the jacket to reveal all that lay hidden behind. It seemed like everyone were all at a live taping of the Arsenio Hall show or something. Everybody in the place pumped their fists in the air in a thrill of excitement, as they cheered her on. It was surely a sight to see without a doubt.

The part that really got the boys to their feet was when Yola snatched her shirt off to reveal those beautiful breasts of hers. They were covered with rose petals. She ripped her pants off, and all hell broke loose. She hit a backwards handstand, then did another split onto the floor.

Parlay had to look around to witness the effect she had on the crowd. *Un-fucking-believable*, he thought to himself. Yola Sweetz had the crowd under her spell. It was evident that she was a master at her craft, and Parlay had to admit, he was more than turned on by the sight of her and how hidden was the G-string between those plump ass-cheeks she flaunted. At that moment, he'd come to realize exactly why she was so valuable to the business, and equally important to Mr. Raymond. There had been so much motherfuckin' money thrown onto the stage by the time Yola Sweetz's set was over. Parlay desired to give her her due props. She was by far the best performer he may had ever seen.

Following, he was determined in his own views, to get with her even more so moving forward. He saw opportunity and financial gain from a strong and solidified bond he'd envisioned developing. The only duty for him would be to find a way to steal some of her friendship from Mr. Raymond. In a good way obviously. And then build something from the ground up, to silently rival that of R.E. Stephens management. Nothing like healthy competition in a busy business. Parlay did have a right to become a competitor. But he badly needed to get his money right to be appealing in a major way.

Parlay knew that such transition would not go down without an epic battle with and bloodshed. Or death even. At least that was what his street instincts suggested. His street assumptions tossed out others. Strictly for debate in his own mind. It was as if there were two high class and highly decorated pimps jousting for the possession of a top money-making girl to add to their stable. One was new to it. And the other was true to it.

Parlay was yet again yanked back to reality by a disturbance near the restrooms. As he made his way down the stairs in the direction of the problem, he noticed Big Mix en route to the same to assist. A few of the customers had made a speedy exit out the club. Parlay and a few other bouncers swarmed the area. One of the aggressors landed an extra three piece to the jaw of the guy he had the altercation with. The blows didn't seem to faze dude, because he fired back quickly with a few blows of his own, to the face and the head of his opponent. The security team rushed in to subdue them both. One of the bouncers had applied a little more pressure in his choke-hold than required of him.

"What the fuck you trying to do, my nigga, kill me or something!" the choking victim said to Bo Jack.

The second guy mule-kicked his aggressor directly in the nuts before we were able to fully subdue him.

"Alright, buddy! Yo' ass better take it easy up in here, before this shit gets ugly real fast, playboy!" Big Mix stated.

The crew escorted them out the club and to their cars before going back inside.

"I'm glad to see y'all dealt with that quickly," Yolanda said. "But other than that, what you think about my set?" she asked of Parlay.

He looked down into her face and gazed directly into those beautiful eyes she had. "Damn, girl. I didn't know you had it like that. It was off the chain. I loved it."

"You wouldn't be pulling my leg, would you?"

"Trust me, sweetie, you got a few niggas up in here with damp boxers on after watching you. They're bustin' on themselves, literally."

"Boy stop," she stated with a laugh.

"I'm dead-ass serious, Yolanda. You had these motherfuckas under your spell. And from the looks of the money you piled up, they showed their appreciation too. Rightly so."

She stood mute for a moment before speaking again.

"I was thinking that if you don't have nowhere to be, or if you ain't got to rush home to someone, I would like to treat you to breakfast."

"Hey, that sounds good to me. What time we talking about leaving here tonight?"

"Don't worry. I won't leave without you," she said with a smile. "I don't mind spending some of this money on a meal."

Chapter 11

Roughly two hours later, Parlay was summoned to report to Mr. Raymond's office. Big Mix was the escort, as always. Once inside the domain, Parlay took notice that the boss was on the verge of calling it a night. He had his silver briefcase handcuffed to his left wrist and his pistol in his right hand. Sitting his pistol on top of his desk momentarily, he reached into the inner pocket of his suit to retrieve a small manila envelope. It was a little larger than the ones in the church that sat within the collection plate. First, he handed it to Mix, then from Mix to Parlay. It was his payment for services rendered thus far. The envelope was thick and flushed with money.

"I hope you find it to be a generous pay for your services here at King of Dimez, young man. Although not yet a full-time member of the K.O.D. Family, nonetheless you're part of the team. And I'm sure you'll become family at some point in the future."

"You know Mr. Raymond, after doing almost twenty years of my life in a prison cell, and this being the first payment I've received since I've been free, it's more than a generous amount. It's a blessing. And on top of that, I'm ready to work hard enough and grind my way up the ladder to truly be living. The only hard part I find about the job, for some dudes I would think, but not me, is maintaining sexual discipline. I've worked my way through desires and impulses, and continuing to hold control of my manhood and not thinking with the little head. But outside of the job, any one of these sexy females can get it. That's it. That's all I can think of," Parlay replied.

Mr. Raymond couldn't help but find humor in the remark made, as they all shared a laugh together.

As the men exited the office and made their way to the balcony of VIP, Mr. Raymond extended his hand to shake Parlay's once more. Yolanda graced the scene.

"So, I take it that this is the beginning of a beautiful working relationship," she stated.

"Well Yolanda, you know me, it's all business on my end, baby-girl. Not only that, it really depends on your friend here. If the ship sails the wrong way, we could always slide one out and pull one in at will. But I honestly believe Mr. Melvin here will work out just fine," Mr. Raymond stated and patted Parlay on the shoulder as he stepped off, on his way out the door to go home presumably. He was allowed the final words for the night.

—

Parlay made it his business to ask Big Mix what time he needed to report to work daily? Mix told him to show between 8:00 and 9:00. He also let him know that he had the option for two days off. Parlay chose Sundays and Mondays.

"That's funny how you *and the one who referred you,* have the same off days," Big Mix stated.

"Why you find that odd?"

"I just do."

Parlay somewhat detected heavy shade but downplayed it.

Yolanda heard what Mix had said but acted as if she didn't. After Mix left, she and Parlay looked at another in their attempt to try at making sense of Mix's remark. Big Mix had agitated the man.

"Yo, what was that all about?"

"You know Melvin, it really does hurt some dudes to their poor little hearts and cause great pain to their ego, for them to shoot their best shot at a woman, only to be turned down. That's what his smart-ass remark was all about."

"So, you were listening, huh?"

"Of course, I was. I believe he has a problem with the fact that I was willing to stick my neck out for you. But I know determination. And that was what I observed in you.

"So exactly what was you doing at the airport that day we met?" Parlay had to ask of her.

"I had just returned from Atlanta visiting family and taking care of some business of mine. I felt that it would be a win-win situation for he and I—Mr. Raymond that is—being that he needed a man, and I had the go ahead to find him that person outside of the knowledge of Big Mix. Mr. Raymond again, I'm referring to. I do have the ear of the boss. And that's another part Mix can't stand," she further explained.

"Okay-Okay-Okay, I get that, you got more pull and clout with the boss than one of his most trusted bodyguards on certain matters. Why do you feel the need to instigate or not speak up when necessary, when negative statements are made like the one not long ago?" Parlay questioned.

"How else would I get to know the ways and the underhanded mentality that these dudes possess if I don't allow them the opportunity to personally incriminate themselves? And, I have to stick my head out there for you. I was the one to refer you, so I got to make myself look and sound good, right? Besides, that's what friends are for. I'm sure you are aware of this," she stated.

"True."

"Alright then, that's all you need to be aware of at this particular time," she said, concluding on the matter and batting those beautiful thick eye lashes of hers.

Yolanda flexed on him with her strut and sassy demeanor as she walked off in those tight-fitting stretch pants she had on. The kind that allowed her ass-cheeks to clap back in a sensational fashion. Parlay knew there was an absolute need to keep a strong level of control at all cost. He couldn't give in and pursue her, because that would be bad for business. Business was more important than anything else at that point.

He managed to catch up to her, matching step for step.

"Yo, you go right ahead. I'll be out there shortly. I need to stop by the bar for a moment," he said to her.

"You go right on. I'll wait for you," she replied.

Parlay originally changed into his security outfit there at work at the start of his shift. Along with an extra pair of gloves, a few sport drinks, and a hat, the button down he wore was left at the bar behind the counter, as he'd placed his protein shakes and bottled water in the refrigerator to keep cool.

Tisha was tallying up her register when he walked up. He asked of her to pass him his belongings.

"I got you Melvin. Just give me a minute or two, please. I don't want to lose count. Those dudes are serious about their money. And I'm serious about mine . Also my job. It has to be all calculated and accounted for," she said. "Thank you for being patient."

"No problem. I understand."

She wrote something down on a paper napkin and then took advantage of the opportunity to make small talk with the new attractive guy.

"So, you think you're cut out for this line of work and not get seduced or attached?" she asked specifically of Parlay.

He'd read between the lines and understood what she was hinting at. A smile stretched across his face. "Why don't you ask me the same in a few months. If I'm still here."

Tisha returned the smile and made it a point to walk from behind the counter to get up close and personal. She now stood face to face while handing him his property. The way she fitted those pink stretch pants and those expensive pumps she had on. Tisha really stimulated dude in a major way. She'd caused an erection. Not to mention the enticing gap she had between her legs. Shortly had a camel-toe like no other. Her private was puffed and screamed seduction.

"Here you go," she said with a smile, licking her lips in the process. "Now, if and when you get the urge or feel the need to have a good woman in your life that definitely knows how to cater to a man and treat him—even down to the point of being sure that his shirt stays crisp and neatly folded as he performs his duties at work—don't be afraid to give me a call, okay?"

She smiled and handed over the shirt, along with the other things he'd situated in her area.

She then extended her hand with a napkin pinched between the index finger and thumb as she offered it to him. Parlay opened his hand, and Tisha pressed the napkin gently in the palm and stroked the back of his hand as she eased hers away. He took the napkin, folded it neatly, and put it away into his pocket.

"I got you, Tisha. I'll be sure to keep in touch."

They stood in silence smiling at one another and glaring into each other's eyes. She chewed on her gum, frequently licking her lips to add sex appeal to her presentation Parlay inhaled the pleasant smell of spearmint. Tisha must have really been feeling herself, because her nipples were hardened, and peeping at dude through the paper thin body-fitting shirt she wore. Parlay felt the desire to sex her at some point in the near future. But then, backed off from the notion, once it can to mind that she was the daughter of the co-owner of the club.

As he headed to the front door, his energy detected her eyes stayed on him. As bad as he wanted to go back and talk more, he simply couldn't. The choices in females he took a liking to was beginning to be many. He hadn't been out of prison a month yet.

Outside of the club, he looked around for Yolanda. He had no knowledge of what type of car she drove.

Beep-beep!

He turned to observe Yolanda seated behind the wheel of a powder-blue G-series convertible BMW. Stepping in brisk and flare towards the car, the hunger pangs had really begun to hit him.

Once seated, he strapped on the seat-belt, and his nostrils immediately became invaded by the aroma of the herbs. She had blazed up a blunt.

"Damn, sweetie. That shit smells good."

"Strawberry Kush. Nothing but the best," she said.

"I can tell. I can tell."

Yolanda took another toke of the herbs and then put the car in drive and proceeded towards their destination. She exhaled the smoke like a coal-powered early twentieth century freight train. She blew the smoke upward and out the coup. The top was down.

"So, how many sets did you have to perform to get this nice-ass ride?"

Yolanda turned and looked at dude in astonishment. She then smiled with a slight laugh. "Did you really just ask me that?" she questioned. "I'll give you a pass this time, due to the fact you been locked away all those years. I detect you truly don't mean any harm. But let me school you to something. My choosing to embrace you as an acquaintance and potentially build something of a friendship, was strictly a choice that I made, because I saw something in you, and liked what I'd seen. I envisioned that a fresh start for you would be a golden opportunity to help you redeem yourself with the society that you took for granted. But Melvin, not for one time, shall you think of me as a slut, a prostitute, or just as a stripper, okay. I know myself to be a performer, an entertainer, and a professional dancer that makes my cream from the clubbing and exotic industry. And that's how I want and need for you to see me. And also, to know me as.

Because on the real, bro, I don't have to make none of the exceptions for you that I do. And I don't have to share my time with you. But guess what, I do. And I find myself feeling you, until you finally fuck up and show me something different," she stated with a straight face and an occasional glance into his eyes as she drove.

Without a doubt, she had him on that one, because his initial thought was that she had to sell her body or suck on a dick or two on the low, once her hours ended from popping her pussy on stage.

In defense of himself, Parlay said to her, "slow down sweetie. You don't have to bite a nigga's head off, okay. Geez!"

"Wait a minute. Allow me to finish my point," she retorted and continued, "Now, there are definitely times that a girl wants to do her thing no doubt. But, It's not like I go around fucking every dude I encounter, or try to entice every dude that I meet. It just so happens that you turned out to be the best prospect in all that we were trying to do, I believe. Besides, I'm in need of true companionship, and a bona fide male friend. One who can also prove to be an even better business partner."

Yolanda had his full attention as he was captured and moved by the words and the understanding conveyed.

"Oh, so I'm the best prospect huh?" Parlay stated. "Why couldn't it have been that fate, or the 'God of good fortune' had dealt me a good hand?" he further stated with a smile about his face.

She returned the show of affection and didn't speak another word on the subject.

As they pulled into the parking lot of the diner, Parlay said to her, "Since this meal is on you, I'll go easy and not order too much, okay. I don't want to hit your purse too hard," he joked with a smile.

"Just be sure to save enough room for dessert, playboy. You can't finish a meal without something sweet to eat."

Chapter 12

"Come, Melvin," Yolanda said, once she spotted an empty table. As she led the way, he followed closely behind.

A waitress made her way over to take their orders. Whenever y'all are ready," she said as they looked over menus.

"I'll have two pecan topped waffles," Parlay told her. "Also, a side order of eggs covered with cheese, an order of turkey sausage, and a slice of that red velvet cake y'all got on the counter. Oh yeah, a nice hot cup of coffee too, please. Don't worry about the creamer and the sugar. Just straight like it is, please."

It was now Yolanda's turn. "And I would like the steak dinner with eggs," she said. "Add cheese to my eggs also, and include a side of toast to go along with that. Coffee for me as well."

The two sat quietly for a few minutes, up until Yolanda spoke out in excitement. "*Ooh!* Take a look at that!"

Parlay turned in time to witness the Cuban chef putting on one hell of a show as he prepared the orders of food. He twirled and chopped while dashing and flipping the seasoning shakers. That dude was like a ninja. It was clear that he was a master grill operator.

"Man, that was nice," Parlay acknowledged.

"I thought you would like that," Yolanda said.

"That dude should be somewhere doing his own thing."

"Yeah. I've been telling him the same thing for months," she said.

Their conversation continued, and they covered many topics while talking. When the food arrived, no time was wasted to dig in. They both had a huge appetite.

—

Meanwhile . . .

Meanwhile, on the far end of town, seated in the back of his Rolls Royce Phantom, Mr. Raymond was en route to a high-stakes poker game that was being hosted by one of his old-school business partners and friend. The driver for Mr. Raymond that night was a personal bodyguard as well and a friend. He was a slim, silent guy named Willie.

Also, along for the ride was Cherniece, one of the former dancers from the club he'd kept close to him. She was a twenty-six-year-old, caramel complexioned beauty with a nice figure, a big booty, and from good stock. She also served as one of Mr. Raymond's play things when he wanted to be with her in that way.

Mr. Raymond felt comfortable talking business in front of her. He was engaged in a phone conversation with some big shot and revealing his thoughts on exiting the club scene to enter politics at some phase eventually.

"Yeah, man. You know I've been engaged in talks with a few people. I let them know I've been heavily thinking about the prospects of putting together a decent campaign team, and take my best shot at seeking to become the Mayor of this great city. Miami can really use an intelligent deal maker of a black man to lead the town."

"Right on, brother," a deep-voiced man replied.

" No doubt. And since Obama left office, Kasim Reed got voted out as Mayor of Atlanta and was replaced by a bitch, and Minister Farrakhan getting too old to continue his post, there ain't too many solid black men out there to be representatives of black political thinking."

"You're right, Ray. I never saw it like that before."

"Hell, I figured that, wherever Mayor Dinkins failed at in New York City during his tenure as Mayor, and wherever Marion Barry fucked up in the Nation's capital, I can make right and redeem the black Mayoral figure here in Miami-Dade. Kwame Kilpatrick turned out to be simply too corrupt. And that stupid-ass nigga Ralph Naggins over in New Orleans did too. I could go on and on with my disdain. But yeah, that's what the plan is, Rich. So it seems for right now. I'm going to give that club shit up and move on into politics. I got to find a few people to assist me though. I also got to find a way to cut a few people out of the loop, in order to get top dollar once I sell the club. I think my time has come and gone for that shit. I got enough young pussy in my stable to keep me alive and going well into the next life to come," he said and aggressively grabbed Cherneice by her right thigh, then groped her between the legs.

"You're a visionary, Ray. I believe in you, my brother. I know you can do it," Richard stated.

"Yeah, man. I believe I can too. It's just going to have to be a lot of heartbroken motherfuckers that's going to be pissed at me. Especially Mitch. But, I've got to do what I've got to do. I've got to carve out a lot of people from my circle. I might create enemies, but shit, it ain't like I can't deal with that too. Suit up, Rich. Shit may get real."

Mr. Raymond contemplated over a way to get the thirty percent stake of the club back from Mitch he held, and also, on how to terminate the contract he'd agreed to with Yolanda. There were certain clauses in the contract that mandated part ownership and percentage payment of the K.O.D. brand, which would exclusively go to Yolanda for copyright purposes. Also, Yolanda maintained a percentage for dancers that she brought into the club.

Indeed, Mr. Raymond had dirty laundry to air out and a few cutthroat policies had to be employed. He also had reason to be weary and possibly fearful of those that may be offended by the process. Nonetheless, his intentions was to simply cut bait and move on about life how he saw fit for himself and his family.

—

Back At The Diner . . .

As the two enjoyed the last few bites of the meals they ate on, the both was briefly interrupted by a female whom had raced over to their table.

"Girl! How you been? I wasn't quite sure if it was you or not sitting over here looking so ghetto fabulous. And mind you, with this handsome man by your side."

"How are you, girl? Long time. I thought you moved some place out of town," Yolanda mentioned to her good friend, a female named Rachel. They'd met years ago, after Yolanda recruited Rachel to dance at King of Dimez.

"I did. But we definitely need to catch up soon," Rachel said with a smile.

"How about tonight? We were just about to leave."

Yolanda introduced Rachel to Melvin and they conversed briefly before exiting.

Chapter 13

Weeks Prior . . .

Midway across the Southern part of the country, at a safe house in Houston, Texas, an intense conversation took place between Santino Bubbs, aka "S. Bubbs" and his young gun runners he had out and about on a mission for him. They'd been sent to fulfill a couple of contracts that their boss and leader had out on the life of a few whom had gravely violated one way or another. The targets lived in South Florida. Miami and Fort Lauderdale in particular.

"Look you two, y'all either calling me to report one thing or another," S. Bubbs declared, "a detailed description of the scenario that's about to play out because you've found that bitch Rachel and about to put her lights out; or, you're hot on her trail? Now which is it?" S. Bubbs demanded to know.

"Nah, Bubbs. That's not exactly what the temperature is down here in sunny, southern Florida. We just checking in with you to make the fact known that we made it to our destination and have gotten in contact with a few people that know the hoe. They say she use to strip at one of the clubs down here, the one called King of Dimez. And she may still be at it. They suggested that we check there as well," one of the young dudes said.

"Yeah, I'm familiar with that spot. That's where I met the bitch. But fuck all that! What other info you got on that bitch?" he inquired.

Bubbs seemed to get more agitated at the fact that his boys had not caught up to the bitch yet. Indeed, he needed the two hitters to get to her, long before she made it to the police, or before she'd done otherwise with the valuables she had stolen from him.

"You listen to me and y'all listen good, my nigga! I don't give a flying fuck about what you got to do or how you got to do it! Y'all get me that thieving snitching bitch Rachel ASAP! And make sure she doesn't live to enjoy the shit she's done! The last thing I need is for the bitch to steal $400,000 from me, and also, have to look up at the bitch on the witness stand testifying against me in the courtroom! That bitch subject to sing like she's a member of the Mississippi Mass Choir, if we don't permanently muzzle her first. You get my drift. Now, do work like I know y'all capable of doing, my nigga! And where Bill at?" S. Bubbs further demanded to know.

"He right here," the young partner in crime replied. A silence came about as the device exchanged hands from Lil C-Boy to Wild Bill.

"Yeah, boss. What you got?" Wild Bill asked.

"It's been a slight change of plans, cowboy. Once y'all get the right amount of information to be able to get at that bitch when the time is right, I need for y'all to take a trip just north of Miami to Fort Lauderdale. Hit this number when you get there. It's to a nigga named Marco. At one point, he was cool with some niggaz named Bam and Spanky. It's those two who's responsible for killing one of my cousins down there about a year ago. They ended up falling out with Marco and then turned and robbed him. They badly pistol whipped the man after their group split. Now Marco switched up on them and exposed all he knew about the killing of my cousin to another family member I got down there. Those past bad deeds of them two motherfuckas' Bam and Spanky, is about to come back and bite them niggaz right in the ass. Like the 'good book' says, there is no bad deed that goes unpunished.'

I got to see to it that that pussy-ass nigga Bam gets it, for real. Because he the main one. And if that nigga Spanky so happen to be with him when he gets touched, he gets it too. But Bam the target. Like I say, if you could get two for the price of one, then that's better. But if only one, that'll work too, you hear me on that? I got two last words for you on; *lights out*! No questioned asked, my nigga! Just go to work." S. Bubbs affirmatively stated.

"For sho," Wild Bill replied.

"Here's the number. Lock it into your phone so you don't have to call me back about it. It's nine-five-four, eight-eight-three, one-seven-zero-three. That's the contact to the nigga there. He wants them niggaz knocked off probably more than I do. Remember, Marco. And you calling him for me, S. Bubbs, out in the Fifth Ward, H-Town. He'll know from there what the lick read. I'm out," S. Bubbs stated and ended the call.

Bill and C-Boy knew that their boss would reward them big time for the additional delivery of heads that they put on a plate and dropped off to the grim reaper. The details and new set of instructions had been related, and the duo hit squad went on to carry out their work and paid duties.

—

Presently . . .

That night after the meal at the diner, Yolanda dropped Melvin off at home and was situated at her own place along with her friend, Rachel. The two didn't experience any form of tiredness nor sleepiness. They'd intended to stay up all throughout the night and early wee hours of the morning talking and discussing ways to resolve the troubles that Rachel feared.

"You really got yourself a nice place here, Yolanda. It's a huge step up from that shoe-box you once called home," Rachel said with a laugh at her own words.

Taking the comment with a grain of salt and not being offended in the least by the sarcastic laced remark, Yolanda felt obliged to respond. "Yeah, girl, I've really gotten both my feet firmly planted and elevated my game to get out of that one-bedroom shack I previously paid rent to live in. I still can't believe I used to pay to be in that house," Yolanda said.

She then placed a batch of chocolate chip cookies and two glasses of milk on the table for them to snack on and reminisce of the glory days that they shared in the stripping business.

Rachel was now 36 years of age and still thought that she was 26, being that she'd maintained a nice fit body, ass, and thick set of thighs. She had a slight pudginess to her gut, but overall, she was passable as a good potential sex partner and still capable of selling pussy or a blowjob to her would be customers.

"Bitch, you still eating those damn chocolate chip cookies and drinking milk to wash them down, ain't you?" Rachel stated is a surprised type of way.

Taking a seat down on the couch and beginning to munch on her snack, Yolanda attempted to get Rachel to open up. "So, what's going on that got you so scarred and twisted to the point that you fear for your life being in danger?"

"Girl, I really got myself in some serious shit this time, you hear me," Rachel said and began to shed tears once more. Yolanda retrieved the box of Kleenex from the end table and passed it to her friend. Wiping her tears and blowing her nose in the process, Rachel gathered herself as she readied to relate the troubles she faced.

"Let me start from the beginning, okay. The reason I left Miami is because, I had met this guy that had been visiting. We met at the club one weekend. He was from Texas. I really thought he was the one, because of the level of maturity he displayed, and him being a few years older than me. Truth be told, this nigga had shit on lock out there in Houston. And you know how I am about a nigga with money that knows how to show a bitch the finer things in life and treat a bitch accordingly. He was a sugar-daddy by all means and the type of man I needed, that someone who was real generous with their money," Rachel said.

In a vain and sarcastic fashion, Yolanda replied, "Yeah, I *already* know how you like to front and put on the way you do."

"My people tried to warn me about moving out of town with a man that I didn't know all too well, but I refused to listen. I figure that they were only jealous and hating on a bitch and didn't want me to outshine them as I was to come back and visit. It was no sooner than I had moved out there and into the large home he owned that a bitch had really began to feel large and worthy of being treated like royalty," Rachel related.

"Get the fuck out of here, girl!"

Yolanda waited for her to say more.

Rachel continued, "Yeah, girl, I don't want to sound like I'm exaggerating anything, but nobody could tell me shit, you hear me. From lavish house parties to premier club events, to VIP treatment of every place we visited, we did that. I tell you, if that nigga wanted it, he had it. One of his brothers was one of them big-time hip-hop music moguls that owned a record label, and he had money tied into that, among other things," Rachel said.

Puzzled beyond reality, Yolanda then asked, "If things were going so well, what went wrong? Why do you fear for your life now? Why are you hiding from this guy?"

Enjoying a bite from one of her cookies and taking a swig of milk, Rachel said, "Damn, girl. These some banging-ass cookies you got here."

Yolanda gave her a look from hell that said it all.

"Now is not the time to keep bullshitting me, Rachel. Now ain't the fucking time, okay!"

"Okay, Yolanda, here we go. No more playing," Rachel said and then cleared her throat. "Now, I know he was in the game. And heavy too. But, what I didn't know, was how deep in the game and connected that the nigga was. Hell, I didn't care at all about him being out and putting his dick in every bitch that the Lone Star state—or is it *Longhorn* State, whatever—had to offer, so long as the nigga took good care of me as he had satisfyingly, and didn't bring any drama my way or a disease, you hear me. Anyway, one night, that arrogant and conceited bastard had the nerve to come home with two bona fide sluts with him that he'd picked up at a club, thinking that he was about to have his way with us all," Rachel revealed.

"Oh, no the fuck that nigga didn't, girl!" Yolanda responded.

"No, girl . . . let me finish. At the point of me stepping to him and demanding to know why in the fuck he thought it was cool to try and play me like that, the nigga then began to beat me terribly bad, like I was his worst enemy or something!" Rachel said and pointed to a few of the wounds that were permanent and still visible, like the scars over her eyes and on the bridge of her nose suffered from the punches.

"Girl, those skank-ass bitches who was with him didn't even try to help me, break it up, or say one word. They just stood there and watched as if they had tickets to a UFC title bout between a pimp and his bottom-bitch! I would have thought that women shared a strong and unbreakable bond like no other, but obviously not," Rachel stated.

Suddenly, Yolanda burst into laughter. "Damn, Rachel! I'm sorry, girl. I had just imagined the look on the faces of those poor girls once it dawned on them that indeed, they were the ones responsible for you getting the hurts put to you," Yolanda said.

"You know! I never looked at it that way, now that you said it," Rachel said and then laughed at the thought herself.

"But keep going, girl. I know it's more to it than that. You don't fear for your life because of that, I know," said Yolanda.

"That is not all of it. The serious part is this. I was a witness to a murder that my boyfriend and another guy by the name Wild Bill, had committed," Rachel stated in a somber tone.

"What! I know the fuck you didn't just tell me no shit like that, Rachel! Are you fucking serious!" Yolanda shouted in a demanding voice to eliminate any further bullshit.

"Yeah, I'm serious. They took another man's life in cold blood right there before my very eyes," Rachel declared.

"Why didn't you call the cops or go to the them for help?" Yolanda asked?

"I couldn't. I was too afraid."

"What!"

"I'm serious as a heart attack, Yolanda. I was too afraid. I felt it wouldn't be too much longer before he was to have someone come to kill me too. I'm gonna die, Yolanda. Die. Do you hear me?" Rachel stated. Tears welled in her eyes once again as she related what she felt her fate would eventually become.

"How you figure he gone come to kill you too? You got away, didn't you? And not only that. I want to know why you never went to the police with this information," Yolanda said.

"I know he's got it out for me, because once we got home that night after we left the spot where they killed the guy at— Carl, that was the name of the guy who was murdered— Santino pressed the gun in my face as he swore on the soul of his two daughters, that he would blow my motherfucking brains out, if I said anything about what I'd saw. And especially if I ran to the police. He said to me, '*Bitch! You know I got connections all over this city and in other states. And if I find out you said anything to anybody, I'mma kill you my motherfucking self, if I'm able to get my hands on you. Now play with it! Play pussy and get fucked, bitch!'* He repeated himself over and over with his threats to me. They were on more than one occasion. And at the time I had planned my escape, I would act like I'm on Facebook or something else, or like I'm texting a girlfriend. But in all actuality, I was recording him on my phone with his threats and forwarding the saved material to my email in the event something did happen to me, or I came up missing. At least I had a witness to my disappearance," Rachel made Yolanda aware.

"Good. At least you had the sense to do that. But what about this murder part you made mention of? What actually happened? And what did you see?" Yolanda questioned.

Rachel took a long pause before responding. There was something she felt the need to say.

"Damn! Girl, if I didn't know any better, I would've thought you were the fucking feds with the way you asked those questions," Rachel replied. "But anyway, this is what happened. Santino had a second house out in the country on the outskirts of Houston in the Woodlands Area, a safe house slash stash spot for his large supply of cocaine. It was his laboratory, so to speak, where he weighed, cooked, and packaged his product. We stayed in that house off and on over the course of two years during the time we were together, and I was very accustomed to Wild Bill being there every so often. He and another guy that tagged along with him."

"They would be there with Santino handling business and chilling out at times. On the day that the murder occurred, Santino called Carl over to the house saying that they may be able to discuss some business and to strengthen the ties of the family. Santino had to lure his intended victim over. Santino lied to Carl by telling him that he and Wild Bill were to be his two closest workers, and that no one else on the team held more rank than his top lieutenants, those two. Being taken by the gesture, Carl knew that he was one of very few people that were ever to be invited to the house, and that there would be nothing but the four of us there that day, Santino, myself, Wild Bill, and Carl once he showed. I was used as a decoy to ease the fear Carl may have held. But, there we were, all four of us seated at the dinner table, sipping an expensive champagne and discussing all that the business was to be. I kept silent for the most part, as Santino did the talking, like always. Next thing you know, Santino got up and began to walk in circles around the table as he lectured about what the plans were for the team and the position that everyone was to play. Behind the chair against the wall where Carl sat, there was a shelf that had a large painting displayed. Santino had placed a hammer there unknowing to me at the time. As Santino slowly walked and lectured with his glass in his hand, he stopped directly behind Carl and then turned and reached around the picture to grab the hammer that was there. I had no idea what was going on or what was about to happen. Santino and Wild Bill plotted to kill the boy on that night. Lord knows I didn't know shit. Suddenly, Santino turned to face us with his hands behind his back and the hammer gripped tight while continuing to lecture. He was still behind Carl. With a lot of force, Santino raised the hammer high above in the air and then came down with it, busting Carl in the top of the head, causing blood to splatter every which way on top of the glass table. He hit him five more times on the head as he lay out cold."

Rachel related the horrific incident to Yolanda in morbid details while she cried uncontrollably.

She continued, "That wasn't the end of it, Yolanda. As Carl stained the table with his blood pouring out his head, Santino ordered Wild Bill to go get the knives that he had. And then, he and Santino began to stab that poor boy over and over again. Santino picked up the hammer once more and beat Carl with it on the head. I guess to be totally sure he was dead without a doubt. An overkill by all standards if you asked me. I just sat there in my seat in absolute shock at all that happened before my very eyes. I put my hands on top of my head and held my mouth wide open as I remained paralyzed from fear. Santino ordered me to take my ass in the bedroom and close the door behind myself as they began to clean up the mess that was made. They ripped up the rug and rolled Carl into it. The glass table was taken out, and the wallpaper had been peeled off. Basically, everything that they needed to do to clear the place of any evidence being left behind had been taken care of. At the point of us leaving the house, Santino and I went one way and Wild Bill had went another in a minivan with Carl's body."

"Over the course of a full week, I was severely threatened to the point of not being able to take it any longer. I couldn't continue to live in fear like that, so I waited until he finally left the house one day to go on one of those business runs that he occasionally took and would be gone for three to five days at a time. I packed up my shit, took all the money and the jewelry that the nigga had in the safe, and I hauled ass girl, you hear me. I went out to California at first, since I got family out there. I laid low for about four months in the hopes that he would give up the chase trying to track me down or had become fearful that I went to the police with all that I knew of his criminal activities and the murder of that poor boy Carl. I just wanted to get the fuck away and allow my life to get back on the right side of living, in a normal sense as it was before I met Santino Bodaford a.k.a. S. Bubbs," Rachel declared.

There was no doubt about it, Yolanda jad to offer something in response.

"Look, Rachel, this is some deadly shit you done found yourself caught up in, girl. And I mean some serious and dangerous shit! I'm very concerned for my own life at this point, now that you've related all of the facts and details of a fucking murder to me. My ass in some deep shit right along with you! And not only could you turn out to be the key witness against that guy in a potential death penalty case, you stole the man's money and his jewelry!" Yolanda affirmatively stated.

"Girl, I don't give a fuck about none of that shit! I had to get the fuck out of dodge, because I knew that the nigga was subject to kill me too before long, being I had seen and knew too much. In the aftermath of them killing Carl, the only thing Santino would do was fuck me, beat the shit out of me, and threaten to kill me, so I figured that the crazy bastard would eventually deliver on his promise if I stayed around. Hell, had I not packed up and ran, I probably wouldn't be here talking with you to this day. As a matter of fact, I know I wouldn't be alive. That crazy motherfucker would always say as he threatened me, 'No face No Case', or 'No witness no chase!' Shit, the only reason the bastard had not killed me was because he used to fuck me every day, and the pussy was too good to him," Rachel said with a laugh to add humor and to make light of a deadly predicament.

"Look Rachel, if anything else, what do you know of the motive that Santino had to kill Carl? What was the reason?" Yolanda inquired.

"I don't really know. I can't say one hundred percent. All I do know is that I overheard some phone conversations about some drugs that came up missing out of one of his shipments. Carl was the main person to be accused of stealing from him. He and some other guy by the name Leon. I don't know what became the fate of him, since I had only saw him maybe once or twice," Rachel stated.

"Okay, and exactly how much money did you take, and how much was the jewelry worth?" Yolanda asked.

"I counted $400,000. And the jewelry—watches, necklaces, bracelets, and rings—I had it all appraised. It was worth $181,000 total," Rachel replied.

"You took $400,000 in cash and $181,000 in jewelry? Girl! That's a $581,000 hit you got out on you! Your ass in big trouble, you hear me!" Yolanda proclaimed.

Rachel reached into her bra to retrieve something. "Promise me you'll hold onto this right here? And if anything, you'll be sure that my son and two daughters and my family gets everything that's left behind for them?" Rachel stated and then attempted to pass Yolanda a key that she let dangle from her fingers.

Yolanda jumped to her feet and began to pace back-and-forth.

"Girl! I don't know if I want to get involved in this shit! It could cost me my own fucking life by helping you out!" Yolanda stated.

Rachel then jumped to her feet and began to pace herself. "Girl, you got to trust me," Rachel declared.

"Trust you! Please! Your ass is in too much deep shit as it is! And you want me to trust you! Ain't no way!" Yolanda shouted.

"You have to Yolanda. You simply have to. I ain't got nobody else to turn to. Plus, if I were to eventually be killed, who am I to entrust to turn in certain things to the police for me, and also to deliver other materials to my kids?" Rachel asked as she tried to make sense of how dire her situation was to Yolanda.

"What does that key go to?" Yolanda inquired.

"It's to a safe deposit box out in LA," Rachel answered.

"To a safe deposit box out in LA?" Yolanda repeated her words.

"Yes girl, to a safe deposit box out in Los Angeles California," Rachel replied.

"What all is there inside the box?"

"Well, for starters, I got $250,000 in it, three watches, three diamond rings, three bracelets, two thick diamond necklaces, an iPhone that has those recordings on it, photos on it, and a SD card that has many other photos of Santino and I on it. I also got a photo ID of Santino in the box, a handwritten note by me detailing the murder and other activities of Santino, a photo ID of myself, and last but not

RELENTLESS GOON | PRINCE A. TAUHID

least, I got a sealed plastic bag in it that has a semen sample wrapped in a thick stack of tissue I removed from myself to turn into the police to scream 'rape' on that bastard once the police finally does catch up to his ass and put him away. If he gets lucky and beat those other charges, I would be able to nail his ass on the rape with that DNA sample I kept," Rachel related.

"Look, Rachel! Promise me that when this is all said and done, you'll get your life back together for the better?" Yolanda asked of her.

"Girl, I promise you on that. I can't continue to go on like this. This shit is not safe, and this shit is not healthy," Rachel stated as she handed her dear friend the key to her box that contained overwhelming evidence against her former boyfriend. "You have my word girl," Rachel added.

Once their conversation came to an end, Yolanda began to walk towards her bedroom to finally get the rest she longed for. But right before getting to room, she stopped dead in her tracks and turned to face Rachel to speak a word or two before calling it a night.

"I never told you this before. But girl, I ain't got nothing but mad love for you, my girl. Mad love," Yolanda said.

"And I love you too, Yolanda," Rachel replied.

"Now try not to eat all those damn chocolate chip cookies or drink all of that milk, because it'll do a mean number on your stomach," Yolanda humored.

They both shared a much-needed laugh together.

"Now please get some sleep because after all the shit you told me tonight. We could definitely use it," Yolanda said as she made her way to the master bedroom.

Chapter 14

Two Weeks Later . . .

Parlay found it somewhat mystifying in a way, for a man to be sound asleep and then as he woke up from his deep resting period, he'd have a hard-on. He had always wondered whether God maintained a sense of humor or not in the moment he created a man's sex organ.

As he relieved him self, he felt as though he'd empty all of the fluid from his body. It was like he was a mini fire truck that had a tank full of water.

Thereafter he groomed and got dressed to impress. As he looked through the fridge, the doorbell rang. To Parlay's surprise, it was Ms. Sheila, the long time neighbor from right next door. She and Mrs. Irene were good friends. She had her micro-braids in a ponytail, and her face was glowing. Her overall appearance was on point.

Parlay stood at the door with a tin foil wrapped plate in his hand.

"Well, are you going to invite me in or what?" Ms. Sheila said.

He opened the barred door and sat his plate down briefly. No sooner, he then saw his mother taking bags of groceries from the trunk of Ms. Sheila's car. As she entered, Ms. Sheila walked right on past him en route to the kitchen.

At that moment, Parlay headed out the front door to help them get the groceries.

"Good morning, son. Momma thought maybe you would still be asleep. I know you wasn't in the habit of getting good rest in that place, and I didn't want to disturb you, baby. I'm glad you up though. Now you can get the rest of these bags for us," his mothet stated.

"No problem," the son responded.

Once he'd gotten the last few bags from the car, he and Ms. Sheila took a pause. This was after his mother did so first. Parlay then extended his hand with a $50 tip for Ms. Sheila.

"Melvin, don't be silly," Ms. Sheila said.

"I want you to have it, just to show you how much we appreciate you."

"Boy, I ain't never charged your momma one red cent to take her to Publix, and I ain't about to start now."

"Some gas money, that's all, Ms. Sheila," he further said to her.

"Well, if you insist, then I guess I'll accept it. Thank you," she said as she took the bill.

"I can't even begin to thank you for all you've done," he said to her.

Ms. Sheila looked downward at the floor out of her strong sense of shyness that she tried so hard to not show but was unable to. Parlay lifted her chin to where they locked eyes with each other. "Any man would be lucky to have you by his side, Ms Sheila. You're a good woman. Don't let no one convince you otherwise."

Ms. Sheila gently grabbed him by the hand and caressed it briefly. She appeared to be about to say something that may have been held back but switched up at the very last second.

"I hope you enjoy that plate of breakfast I fixed for you and your mother," she said with a smile before heading back to her car. Parlay's mind really began to churn in thought.

Chapter 15

Twenty-Four miles north of Miami in Fort Lauderdale, Wild Bill and C-Boy now had the drop on their intended target, Javon "Bam" Rogers. They were in the process of getting at that nigga in a vicious way for their leader, S. Bubbs.

"Look, bro, remember, we go in, lay this nigga down, put his bitch-ass to rest, and do a clean job while we at it. A'ight," stated Wild Bill.

"For sho', my nigga. For sho," C-Boy replied.

The dude Marco whom S. Bubbs told them to contact, had provided them with valuable information on the whereabouts and what have you of Bam. He pointed out his trap spot where the guy's baby-momma lived, gave them one of the main phone numbers that Bam could be contacted, and all other relevant particulars. They even had pictures of the nigga from his Facebook profile. The catch-22 to it all was, how well Marco managed to utilize Bam's greed. This desire will get the best of man each and every time.

Even after robbing and severely assaulting Marco with a pistol, Bam still had the audacity to let his guard down against any revengeful act on Marco's part towards him and allowed him to call his phone, place orders of drug supply through him, and meet him at his place of residence. Now how dumb was that on his part? Marco led Wild Bill and C-Boy directly to their sitting duck, Bam, since they had absolutely no problem getting to their guy. They paid Marco off as S. Bubbs instructed for his role in the set up.

The day was a Sunday night in the early wee hours of the morning. Wild Bill and C-Boy were armed with all they needed to go in with on Bam with, whack his ass, and get the fuck out of dodge immediately. The duo was situated in a small thicket of bushes behind the house where Bam lived. They double-checked to ensure that they were properly suited to pull off the hit. The getaway car was parked three blocks from the location. And once they were to handle their business, they would have to get to the vehicle and peel out of the area.

"Yo, you ready, my nigga?" Wild Billed asked.

"I'm ready, playboy," his partner in crime replied.

"Go!" Bill commanded, as they ran to the backdoor of the home.

Boom!

With one tremendous kick, the backdoor was knocked clean apart from the deadbolt that secured it and dangled by one hinge, barely intact. They ran through, going directly to the main bedroom with lightning speed. Marco provided the hitters with a detailed route from the backdoor to the bedroom. He had sketched a diagram to better assist in them getting to Bam before he could get to the awesome fire power and blast back. Bam was a known shooter. Under Florida's Stand your Ground law, he would have every right to begin blasting first.

The two reached the bedroom and caught Bam attempting to race towards the closet.

"Not so motherfucking fast, nigga! Get your bitch-ass down on the floor!" Bill ordered.

He smacked Bam in the face with the heavy metaled Colt .45 automatic pistol. *Whop!*

C-Boy got in on the action by busting Bam on the back of the head with the .357 magnum he palmed, sending their victim down to the floor flat on his knees where he buckled from the blow. The side of Bam's face, and the back of his head was badly split.

"Tie that pussy-ass nigga up, homeboy!" Bill ordered. "Now, I'm going to ask you one motherfucking time, nigga! Where in the fuck is the money and the dope, Bam!" Bill demanded. He mentioned his name to give a false impression that the two may have been some dudes he knew, but the voice didn't quite register.

"Yo, man! Y'all niggas ain't got to do all this shit, you hear me!" Bam pleaded.

"We about to do a whole lot more if you don't tell us where that motherfucking dope and that cash at in five seconds . . . four-three-two . . . ." Bill dictated as he cocked the .45 getting ready to pop a few slugs into the skull of Bam. He and his girlfriend's one year old started to cry as the girlfriend quickly got the baby to hush, granting Bam a few extra seconds to fess up.

"Bitch, you better make that damn baby shut the fuck up before I do! Permanently!" C-Boy declared.

He pointed his gun towards the girlfriend and the baby. He then ran over and smacked the shit out of the girlfriend in her mouth with the Magnum, knocking three of her teeth out. How cruel and heartless C-Boy truly was. But his actions were what he had been groomed to do.

Before Bill or C-Boy were able to smack any of the two again, Bam spoke up, pointed to the location of the money, and also confessed to the whereabouts of the cocaine.

"The money in the Jordan shoe box at the very bottom of the stack. The box got a big red dot on the label that has the size of the shoe on it. Check in it," Bam said in agony and pain.

"See what's up, bro," Bill told C-Boy.

He went into the closet, knocked over the many shoe boxes Bam collected, got to the main one, then pulled it out the pile.

"Two-minutes and twenty seconds," Bill mentioned the time they had been inside. The goal was to be in and out in five minutes or less. They were on schedule with the business.

C-Boy lifted the top from the shoe box safe to discover the dough. "Bingo!" he announced. There were four thick knot rolls of $100 bills, a debit card, a digital scale, and a bundle of rubber bands inside.

"Now, where the work at, nigga?" Bill demanded to know.

Before Bam could utter a word, his girlfriend told them where to locate the drugs. "It's in the large flour bin in the kitchen, down at the bottom," she stated.

With a nod, Bill directed C-Boy to go see what the deal was. C-Boy rushed to the kitchen to search the flour container. He dumped it over onto the floor to discover two and a half kilos of coke properly wrapped in plastic, and thoroughly compressed. He ran back to the bedroom where the hostage situation was ongoing to show Bill his discovery. Bill gave him two-thumbs up.

Remaining silent and directing C-Boy with his hand and finger to put the money and the yayo in the dark-colored pillowcase, Bill looked at his watch again and then down at Bam as he lay face to the floor.

"Hey, Bam," Bill called out.

"Yeah," Bam replied.

"This for my nigga, Big Tex Bodaford. You remember him, don't you?" Bill stated.

Wild Bill placed the pistol flush up to the back of Bam's head and pulled the trigger.

Boom!

He blew off the back of his top and caused his melon to explode.

Pop-Pop-Pop-Pop-Pop!

C-Boy then put four slugs from his pistol in the upper part of Bam's back.

As they began to run out the room, C-Boy pointed the gun in the direction of Bam's screaming girlfriend and then pulled the trigger.

Pop!

He hit her in the upper shoulder area of her right arm causing her to temporarily pass-out.

They ran out the house, across the backyard, through the bushes, and to the car that awaited, leaving Bam dead as a doorknob, and his baby-momma in critical but stable condition. Wild Bill and C-Boy were in and out in four minutes and forty-four seconds. A perfect killing without leaving one drop of evidence. Or maybe not. Who was to say? After all, there is no such thing as a perfect crime. Especially not murder.

But so far so good. They were $70,000 richer, and two and a half kilos deeper into the dope game. The death of S. Bubb's cousin had been avenged, and the time was to come for the most painful thorn in his ass to be plucked away and wiped out. That was that bitch, Rachel.

—

"Yeah-yeah-yeah! Oh, hell fuck yeah! Right there, baby girl. Stay right there. Keep going . . . keep going . . . Don't stop at all. Faster . . . go faster for me, baby. Ooh shit . . . I'm about to cum, sweetie. I'm about to cum. Here we go . . . here we go, sweetheart. *Ahhh!* Oh, shit, baby. Yeah. Oh yes. Take that. Yeah, take all of that. It's all yours. I want you to have it all. It's all yours, baby."

Mr. Raymond ejaculated at his moment of clarity. He'd released his load in Felicia's mouth, she swallowed every drop of it. She was one of the late twenties early thirties something, short, black, thick, big-booty man-eater and pussy-popping ghetto queen whom he favored, to please him sexually. She was just one of the females he committed infidelity with against his wife, Christine. No one knew of the intimate dealings and affair between the two, other than the personal bodyguards of his, Willie and Big Mix.

Felicia had moved back to South Florida from her second home in Augusta, Georgia when things hadn't been going so well. Originally, she hailed from Fort Lauderdale. Yolanda brought her to K.O.D. and introduced her to the owner to work at his club. Mr. Raymond instantly took a liking to her and all the feminine features she presented, as he saw beneficial to place her in the heavy rotation of girls that serviced him. He was the boss and majority owner of the place. He could do all he pleased, when he was so pleased. Their acquaintance paid off for her from such point onward.

All that was required was she provide him with pleasant and interesting conversation, keep her privacy warm, tight, wet, and satisfying, and give Mr. Raymond a mind-blowing blow job at any time he desired it. Most often, he would get oral sex within the domain of his office at King-Of-Dimez, the self-proclaimed title he gave himself. To him, she performed the best for the time being. As long as she didn't get lock jaw.

Felicia stood to her feet and looked her boss slash lover directly in the eyes with a sinister featured smiled that had the potential to cause Satan himself to give in.

"Was it good to you, daddy?" she asked seductively.

"You got-damn right it was. Good to the very last drop. You got them big full juicy lips on you for a reason, baby-girl," Mr. Raymond stated as he wiped his manhood clean and pulled up his pants, leaving them unzipped and not buckled so he could relieve himself. They both flirtatiously strutted to the bathroom together with her sashaying in front leading the way and him tagging along behind smacking her on the ass with every step to the throne.

As he stood at the sink to wash his hands and her to the side brushing her teeth, he confided in her and revealed the intentions he held.

"Felicia, listen to me, okay. It won't be too much longer before I call it a quits to this club business right here," he stated.

"Oh, really? Why leave it alone? What's next?" she inquired.

"Well . . . for one, I know myself to be far smarter and in possession of great intelligence, not to be utilizing it in a more positive and meaningful way. My father always held a desire for me to donate my life to the service of people. So far so good. But what he truly had in mind, was for me to be of service to the public, not to a bunch of hard dick horny motherfuckas' with a dollar to pitch. That was my idea, to clean up money. But anyway, he groomed me the most over my four other brothers, for a career in some professional field, like a doctor, a lawyer, a senator, a dentist, a judge, or to be a municipal official. He would often say to me, *'son, of the four boys I have—I'm the baby-boy—I prayed and asked God, the good Lord Jesus, to place his personal hand on you and raise you up to be an honorable man, that would someday become a pillar in the community and respectable man in life, earning a living as a professional. That is my prayer and my hope for you, Ray. In Jesus name I pray, Amen. Now son, we got the good part out the way, but the other part you got to keep in mind too. As you progress, you may have to get a little gangster every now and then, ya hear me. In order to make it to the top and maintain at a high level, you got to be two things at the same time, a killer . . . and a King. That's what you must transform into, son. That will be you. You shall be a killer and a King,'* my father willed. I've dabbled with the thought for many years now. Even so before the club thing, which was really not my vision or dream. This is what my oldest brother wanted to do, but he died long before his wish could materialize. I just made it happen on the strength of him, you know. But what my plan is—I think—is that I'm going to get into politics.

I'm going to run for Mayor of this city in the next five years," Mr. Raymond declared.

Now why is this old man telling me all this? I'm not his wife. He need to be letting that bitch know his plans. I'm only here for the money and the other benefits that he got to offer, nothing more. Shit. He only my sugar-daddy and that's it. Why do he seem to think other than? Felicia thought to herself.

"Wow! That's a big transition, ain't it? I'm sure you got what it takes to make it. You cut out for it. But what you plan on doing with the club? It brings in plenty of money, I'm sure. But I know you are aware that club money, ain't good going into the pockets and bank account of a candidate for Mayor or even a potential elected Mayor himself in the eyes of his voters and the taxpayers of the city," Felicia stated.

"You absolutely right, baby-girl. That's why my plan is to sell out and start a different business with the money. Another thing," Mr. Raymond said.

"What's that, daddy?" she asked in reply?

"I'm taking you along for the ride with me," he stated.

"Oh really! You are? That will be so nice, because I'm sick and tired of shaking my ass and titties for a bunch of strangers with a dollar in their hand," Felicia said.

Well damn. This little bitch sounds like the former stripper bitch, Nya Lee, I seen on one of the first few episodes of Love and Hip Hop New York with that statement, Mr. Raymond thought to himself.

"Yeah, sweetie, you got to keep all this to yourself, okay? I mean that. Don't reveal a word to no one, you hear me on that," he stated serious toned so that she would know he meant business.

"Yes, daddy. I most certainly do hear you," Felicia said to Mr. Raymond.

"You know I got to have more than enough trust in you if I'm taking the chance of destroying my home behind you.

107

And also, based on the fact I have revealed what my future plans are to you," Mr. Raymond said to her.

Ain't this a bitch. I haven't even told my wife yet what my future plans are, and here it is I've shared my business with this wench, he thought to himself.

"You mine now, baby-girl. You belong to me. You too good to me to just let go like that. And you ain't got nothing to worry about. I'll see to it you get provided all you want and all you need. The both of us got a lot of work to do in the transition we about to make, and I'm confident we'll do well together."

"That's the spirit, daddy. That is the spirit, sweetie," Felicia replied as they embraced and kissed in the bathroom of the office at the club.

"I promise not to let us down. Trust me on that," Mr. Raymond professed as he fixed his face into a serious demeanor and bit down grinding on his teeth making his jaw muscles flex and bulge out, clearly indicating that he meant business at all costs. Even if that meant bodies had to drop and others were in line to be crossed out. Ray-Ray Stephens felt he had to do what was necessary to be done. His plan was formulated, and the time was at hand for action to take place.

—

"So, let me get this straight, Melvin. I rode years of time with you. I provided you with all that a real bitch was supposed to. And I also did everything else to cater to you. What more could you want or ask for from me?" Traci questioned.

Truth be told, she had dude right there with her, and no other woman had that type of opportunity quite like she did.

"Melvin, I know and understand very well you got a job to do, and it requires you to be there at least five days out the week, long into the wee hours of the night. But for crying out loud, baby. You ain't gave me no true quality time since you been home. And, you ain't fucked me but once. What type of shit is this? Damn! You don't want me no more or something? I ain't attractive to you any longer? My pussy isn't good enough? Is it another bitch or something? What's the problem, Melvin? I need to know," Traci demanded.

"Traci, look here, sweetie, it's not nothing you think, okay. No, it ain't another woman. No, you not ugly or unattractive to me. It ain't none of the above. I'm simply taking my time and proceeding slowly, that's all. I'm not in prison any longer. I don't like to sit around cooped-up in the house all day like I'm still in a cell, and that's what I feel like you want me to do. You work outrageous hours through the week, Traci. So, we not going to have too many days to spend quality time together."

"Melvin, in all honesty, I believe it's someone else, sugar. I'm going to admit, I'm jealous as a bitch. I got trust issues. Like, be for real, Melvin. You got a job as a bouncer at a strip-club, baby. What bitch wouldn't go for a man like you?"

Parlay eased close to her, wrapped his arms around her waist, and lifted her chin so he could gaze into those glory green eyes. He gently kissed her on the lips, to reassure her he wasn't sneaking around.

Parlay had a hard on like his manhood was made from a slab of concrete. He was piped up and ready to roll, and so was she.

Traci mounted and situated her breasts flush against his chest. He palmed her ass cheeks and smacked them twice.

"Melvin, I love you and don't want to lose you."

"Baby, you ain't got to worry about none of that shit on my end. We good. Like I told you, I promise, we good."

"I hope so—"

Her words were cut short. They tongue-kissed in the very moment. He pulled her silk undergarment down to her ankles. She stepped out of them. At the same time, he'd gotten undressed himself.

There they were, naked and fully charged with sexual energy. His dick was inflated and stretched to the max. She spat on his manhood and wrapped those thick warm lips around the head, popping her mouth on the ring of it. Traci tickled the tip with her tongue and began to bob up-and-down, in a freestyle, no hands motion. She then gripped the pipe with both hands and really began to slob on the knob and pull on the dick. Her pace and rhythm were just the way Parlay liked it.

Maybe five minutes into it, he stood to his feet and directed her to get on the bed, on her hands and knees. She grabbed a pillow and placed it under her, arching her back. Her thighs were spread as wide as she could get them to go. The slit between the lips of her private was split open down the center, exposing the fresh and ripe pinkness. He smacked her on the ass hard and then palmed her cheeks, spreading her open. He then glided the dick deep into her life and began pumping and pounding. After an intense interval in easy mode, dude pumped up the volume and began to do his thing.

Parlay ferociously banged Traci's back out doggy-style for a full ecstatic exchange non-stop, without the slightest hint of mercy or remorse. She screamed his name and pleaded for him to fuck her good. And fuck her good he certainly did. He then slowed to control his breathing. Dude inhaled deeply and locked his pelvic flush up against her ass-cheeks meat-to-meat, fully inserted within the chambers of her womb.

Without warning, Parlay released his load, plastering her walls. It felt so damn good to him.

As he slowly pulled out, he relished in the tingling sensation of the aftermath.

"You happy now?" he asked jokingly.

"You damn right, I am," she responded with a smile. "We need to do this more often."

RELENTLESS GOON | PRINCE A. TAUHID

"Relax, baby. I'm home now. We're going to be getting to the business more than you think."

"You got that right, we are! And it's not over with for tonight either. So, you might as well get ready to dick me down again shortly. I definitely want some more from where that came from. You got to keep this strawberry shortcake filled with that thick whipped cream you gush out."

"That's a bet. Let's eat a little something first, and then back to the business."

The two jetted to the kitchen to power-up and munch on grub. After that, it was time round two. Parlay had his work cut out for him sexually dealing with Traci. She was a nymphomaniac in all her glory and beauty

Chapter 16

Two Weeks Later . . .

There are many people who have heard and know the statement to be of truth, that *once a junkie, always a junkie!* It's realistic in a lot of ways, being that the addict who attempts to clean themselves up and get away from the life of drugs seems to keep the same friends they held company with while getting high, and visit the very haunts they previously dwelt within as a free baser.

Similarly, the same applies to a stripper whom wishes to get away from such culture. But truthfully, *once a stripper, always a stripper*. The person that the last statement applied to was Rachel, being that she found herself at the crossroads of having one foot in the game and one foot out. She simply could not leave the life of bouncing her ass, popping her pussy, and wiggling her titties. She had to be involved some type of way.

Even though there were hit men hot on her trail to kill her, she could not give up the life. She'd met Santino in a strip-club, so quite naturally, a strip-club in her hometown would be the ideal place for people to look in search of her.

She'd began dancing at *Love Dolls* on 79th Street NW. Not long before, her application had bee approved for an apartment in Hollywood, Florida.

Rachel stayed the night over at Yolanda's house from time-to-time, and she really didn't know too much about the friend, if anything at all. Yolanda kept her personal life private and well-disguised. The two developed an acquaintance at King of Dimez. That was about it.

At 3:22 a.m., on a Thursday morning, Rachel was spotted leaving Love Dolls. Wild Bill and C-Boy sat shotgun in an all black Ford Crown Victoria equipped with flashing police lights on the dashboard and dark tint to hide behind. C-Boy was at the wheel, and Bill held down the passenger seat.

As Rachel hit the highway, the two killers hopped on the road behind her. C-Boy hit the lights on Rachel for an "improper lane change." She pulled to the side of the expressway and immediately began to hide the open liquor bottle in her vehicle. She retrieved her driver's license, car registration, and insurance card. C-Boy approached the car, perfectly draped in dark clothing. He flashed his light into the driver side rear-view of Rachel's car, temporarily blinding her with the reflection. C-Boy planted himself along the rear end of her car still holding the flashlight.

"I need to see your license and registration, please!" he yelled out.

"Officer, hello sir! How, are you tonight? What have I done wrong?"

"—License and registration, please! After that, I'll be more than happy to tell you why you were pulled over."

Rachel handed over her documents and was advised to remain seated until further instructed.

C-Boy walked back to their car and took a seat.

"Bill, here is our bitch, ain't it? We know she's the right person," C-Boy stated.

"Yeah. It's that bitch! You already know what to do. The plan laid out." Bill reminded him.

"That's right," C-Boy replied. He then re-approached her car.

"Ma'am, I need for you to step out of the vehicle," C-Boy ordered.

Rachel exited and stood with both her hands on her hips.

"What's the problem, officer?" she asked.

"I'm sorry, ma'am. It's a warrant for your arrest on unpaid traffic tickets. I got to take you in to the jail," C-Boy stated and then grabbed Rachel by the wrist placing handcuffs on her.

"What the fuck! I paid those tickets off, I thought!" she screamed and stomped her foot in anger. "What the fuck! Officer, I got the money in my purse in the car to pay off everything right now," Rachel pleaded.

"I'm sorry, ma'am. That won't be possible through me. You'll have that opportunity to do so down at the jail," C-Boy stated, as he quickly escorted her to the rear driver side door of their undercover squad car with her hands cuffed to the back. He knew it was important to hurry and go long before any real officers were to pull up and provide assistance at the scene of the "traffic stop."

Once Rachel was seated and they were on their merry little way, en route towards the Everglades, Wild Bill turned to face her.

"Hi there Rachel! You remember me, don't you!" Bill exclaimed. "Yeah, Rachel! I'm sure you remember me, my girl." Bill turned on the car light to allow her a quick peep at his face.

"What the fuck! Oh shit! Wild Bill! Help! Help me please! Somebody! Anybody! Help me!" she shouted at the top of her lungs.

The inside of the car lit up from the flash of gunfire.
Pop-Pop-Pop-Pop!

Wild Bill pumped four heavy slugs into her body from his .44 Bulldog. She lay on the backseat bleeding badly and near lifeless.

Pop!

An additional shot was fired, as he put a bullet in the back of her head, to ensure baby-boo was no more. Blood oozed from her onto the cloth seats of the vehicle.

They wrapped Rachel's body in black trash bags once in the Everglades. C-Boy dragged the corpse out the car by the legs. He then fired twice with his pistol, putting two hollow-points into the head of an already dead body.

"Take that, bitch! It's for you giving us such a hard time catching up to you!" C-Boy spat at the body of the murdered victim.

The killing duo wrapped the body and secured it with duct-tape. They dumped Rachel in a very shallow area on the marsh land in a pool-sized puddle of water to be feasted on by the many alligators that greatly inhabit the territory. Before leaving, they removed the backseat from the Ford and poured a heavy dose of gasoline on it to destroy the crucial piece of evidence.

As they began the drive out of the Sunshine state back towards Texas, Wild Bill hit S. Bubbs on speed dial.

"Talk to me," Santino answered.

"That thorn you had stuck in your ass, boss. It's been permanently removed," Bill announced.

"Ha Ha Ha Ha!" Santino laughed and smiled in rejoice. "Well done, boys! Good work by the both of you!" S. Bubbs congratulated. "Now, y'all hurry and get back to the house so we can celebrate and bond together as a family. It's deserving."

The name of the game in street politics was chess NOT CHECKERS. Santino knew how to play the board well as he had throughout the forty-nine years of living which he'd existed over the thirty-four and thirty-one years of that of Bill and C-Boy. He'd thought things out well in advance and was several moves ahead of the ambitious opponents that the young gunners were subject to become. If any situation was to develop, he would turn out to be the master who outsmarted his pupils and had laid a trap far ahead of those ungrateful bastards whom he previously dished orders out to. The only other problem S. Bubbs had to deal with from that point, would be revealed soon enough. He had additional unforeseen issues.

—

Parlay had been at home cooling and having a conversation with his mother and taking in the wisdom she always imparted upon him.

"Melvin, baby, you know I only spent a little of the money you left. That was only to pay a bill or two and to take care of a few things your brother needed taken care of."

"Momma, you could have spent every penny of that money if you wanted to. I left it so you wouldn't want for nothing."

"Of course, the settlement allowed me to pay off everything and renovate the house. Other than that, you know your momma ain't a big spender, and I don't care for expensive things. I had my lawyer over the money, and she managed things for me. Now that you're home and in good standing with the law, I'm going to make you my Power of Attorney and put you over everything from here on out. I wanted us to finally discuss this and many other things, and I knew it was best to wait until you initiated the conversation 'bout money. Oh, and the other important thing I took care of out the money was help my first and only grand-baby pay off her student loans and tuition fees. I was willing to put every dime the both of us have left behind that girl and her education. She's real smart. My grand-baby's going to be somebody one day. You mark my words. She too bright not to," the mother said.

"Speaking of Sherita, momma, she came home last night on break from college. She supposed to come by and see us today when she gets up and dressed. We talked yesterday as she was travelling. You were asleep," Parlay mentioned to his mother.

"Oh, she is! the elderly lady let out ecstatically. I can't wait to see my baby," Mrs. Irene responded in excitement.

At twenty-one years of age, Parlay's daughter had grown up on him and was gorgeous as ever. She was enrolled in the

University of Maryland, seeking to acquire a degree in banking and account management. At the time he went inside to prison, Sherita was only four years old. Many years had passed them by. He hadn't seen her and that magnificent smile she possessed in almost two years. All that was about to change.

—

One Day Later . . .
Sherita made it to the home of her grandmother and father. This was to be a well deserved and needed visit.

"Hey, grandma! Hey, daddy!" she greeted and gave the both of them a tight loving hug.

"Hey there, baby. Granny miss you," Mrs. Irene returned the greeting. "Come here and give you grand momma another hug, sugar. I'm so proud of you baby," the old lady added.

"Daddy. Look at you, my guy. You still got that handsomeness about yourself, don't you. And not only that. You got a youthful spirit to go along with it. I truly missed you, man. I really did, daddy," Parlay's daughter said and then began to cry.

"Come to daddy, baby. I love you and miss you too," he said to her and then planted a kiss on her forehead.

At the time when Sherita was eight years of age, something awful and sadistic happened to her. She mustered up the courage to relate to her father that, by him not being there to protect her like a responsible father should, it set the stage for all that went on with her. The girl's life was drastically altered. She was molested by her mother's husband over a period of six years, from eight to fourteen.

Sherita said that her mother Belinda, took sides with Charles. Sherita revealed that, because her mother didn't believe her, she began to feel like it was natural for him to do the things he did. The evil acts were brought to the light, because Sherita had an emotional break while at school one day. She'd begin to break free from the control he had upon her. Parlay wanted to kill that motherfucker! For all the foul shit he'd perpetrated against his precious daughter.

Sherita poured her heart out to her father in those letters she'd written. Parlay badly wanted to do something vicious to Belinda in addition to Charles, for not believing their daughter with all she'd revealed. But Sherita made her father promise not to harm the mother. Belinda never let it get out or allowed the news to reach the ears of those in Miami. It stayed in Jacksonville, where she remained living once her husband went off to prison. Parlay had his mind made up to lie in wait for the first opportunity to have that motherfucker Charles touched. He put it on his life that he would.

"Are you busy later on today, baby?" he asked his daughter.

"No, not really. What's up?" she inquired.

"Oh, nothing too much. Just thought maybe we could go shopping at the mall and enjoy some treats or something afterwards," he related.

"Okay, sounds good to me, daddy. We can do that," she replied.

"How you like my ride out there?" Parlay asked, pertaining to the Tahoe I'd recently bought. A vehicle he'd long desired to have.

"Looks real nice. And it fits you too. It complements your personality and style."

"Yeah. It does, don't it?"

"For real though, it does. Now that you've grown a full, thick beard and buffed up on them weights, I bet you got all the young females thinking you younger than you really are and trying to get with you, huh?"

"You know I got to still be me regardless of who or what, baby. I'm known to be heavily complimented throughout the day," Parlay said.

"Oh, yeah, daddy. I forgot. You did tell me you got a job at a strip-club, right?" she asked with a laugh. "How you keeping all those women off you? And what about Traci? How she feel about your job?"

"Yeah, your daddy got a job at a club. And Traci's cool with it, because it pays well. Now, I'm about to get dressed so we can have our first father-daughter outing, okay."

"Okay, daddy. Take your time. I'm here," sherita stated as she continued to carry on a conversation with her grandmother while her father got prepared.

—

Parlay and his daughter had a really great time together that day, as they utilized the occasion to deeply converse and because acquainted verbally. He made it his business to assure her that she need not worry any further about being hurt ever again, because her father was home, and intended to defend her with his very own life. Even if that meant he had to put ten motherfuckers to rest behind her. He'd do it in a heartbeat. She needed him no doubt, and he needed her.

—

Weeks Later . . .

Everything was appearing to be going well for Parlay on the job. He'd gained a good understanding of the many personalities regarding the people he worked around, and a feel for the females. Whom to talk with and whom not to do so with. At no time did he play close to anyone, because he operated as a loner and was a bit standoffish. Mr. Raymond developed greater trust in him and brought the guy in closer. There were times that Parlay would be worked into the rotation, serving as his personal bodyguard, reporting directly to him. He had also served as Mr. Raymond's driver on a few occasions. There was something about Parlay the individual, that the boss took a liking to. He never mentioned exactly what it was, and Parlay didn't ask. The conversations Mr. Raymond and him would have were always personal and deep. Also, Parlay knew the importance of keeping it real by all means, as he'd sensed a shift in the new set of priorities he now established. To his surprise, Mr. Raymond sought out advice from him, and truly valued the opinion Parlay had given on many matters. It was surreal for Parlay.

Mr. Raymond and him definitely bonded. The boss was big on action and decisiveness, and not so much on words. Dude was the truth, and Parlay looked up to him. The elder of the two became a mentor in a sense. Someone Parlay needed so as to utilize as a model and a standard. Mr. Raymond proved perfect for this particular role.

Chapter 17

Mitch's cellphone rang. He took a look at the screen to identity who it was then answered.

"What's good, Ray?"

"Nothing too much for today. What's good with you?"

"Taking it easy. What's on your mind, my brother?" Mitch inquired.

"We need to talk over a few things. Maybe tomorrow. At one of our favorite spots, The Fountain Bleu. I've got some pressing business that needs to be discuss with you. Four o'clock tomorrow afternoon good time for you?" Mr. Raymond asked.

"Yeah, that's a good time. I've got to go over that way anyhow, to take care of some other personal business."

"Good. I'll see you then. In a minute, bro," Mr. Raymond said.

Mitch stamped by those words by repeating and concluded the call. *"In a minute,"* proved to be a signature way of how the two ended phone conversations.

We ain't held a meeting outside the club in quite some time now, Mitch contemplated. *I wonder what the hell Ray got going on? Or what's he got up his sleeve.* I'll know tomorrow for sure, won't I.

Mitch then decided called his daughter, Tisha, to see how she was doing, and to inquire on other matters.

"Hey, daddy. How you doing?" Tisha answered upon observance of who was calling.

"How you been doing, baby?" Mitch greeted.

"I've been good. What's up with you though? How you been?" she responded.

"Oh, nothing too much. I just got a call from Ray, that's all. He wants to meet up with me tomorrow. He seems enthusiastic and happy about things lately. Also, cautious. And at the same time, he has me in the blind."

"What's the deal?" Tisha inquired.

"I don't know just yet."

"But you say he seems different, right?"

"Yeah. He does."

"Has some of the money turned out to be counterfeit again or something?" she asked.

"No no no, baby. It ain't nothing like that. All the money been legit. And y'all doing a fantastic job. I know Ray well enough to know when he's up to something. And judging from the tone of his voice, I believe that that nigga got something up his sleeve for sure, baby. I got a weird gut feeling about this, Tisha. Everything been going well with the girls on your crew?"

"Yes, daddy. We've been running smoothly." she replied.

"You ain't caught wind of any type of suspicious talk or activities from any of the other employees, have you? Has any of the girls complained of being harassed?" Mitch asked.

"No. At least not that I've heard about. If there was, they would go to Yolanda first. That's *her* area, so, she would be more informed. Although she and I don't necessarily see eye-to-eye on many things, because I don't know or understand her business train of thought nor point of view, due to the both of us never really conversing too much down that lane. She seems to be close with the new guy, Melvin." Tisha said.

"Tisha, well, since you mentioned him, what's your take on him?"

"Oh, Melvin? He's cool. He's straight. Just a tad behind on knowing how to mingle and socialize. But I'm sure that that's due to him being locked up all those years. Other than

122

that, he's good. We talk from time-to-time. He seems to be committed to the job, and focused."

"Baby, you attracted to Melvin ain't you?" Mitch asked with a slight laugh.

"Nah. I do think he's handsome though, and has a nice physique."

"Okay, baby, that's all your daddy wanted to know. Be sure to keep your eyes and ears open. Something's a little fishy here. I'll know soon," Mitch stated.

"Okay, daddy. I will. And I love you too."

"I love you too, baby," Mitch replied and then ended the call.

He continued on about his day now heavily thinking over what Mr. Raymond may was up to.

—

The next day, Mitch was sure to properly drape himself in business attire for the meeting. He was fully prepared for this discussion with Mr. Raymond. At least in mind set and dress. But he never fully knew how to predict the moves and discover the intentions of his friend.

Mr. Raymond's charcoal-gray big body 500 series S-class Mercedes-Benz was parked outside the establishment. Mitch parked, exited his vehicle, and approached the reservation desk.

"Hello, sir! How may I help you?" the maître'd at the front desk asked.

"Yes. Good day. Reservations for Mitchell Collins?"

The gentleman keyed in the information on his monitor and found the name. "Yes, indeed sir. Here we are. I have a Mr. Raymond Stephens awaiting you—"

"Yeah, that's him," cut in to day. He was very eager to be seated at the table and made aware first-hand of what such meeting was all about. He proceeded past the desk en route towards Mr. Raymond. He'd spotted him at a table.

There were faces present that Mitch had never seen before. Raymond sat at the center of the table as he was ready to announce the meeting to be in session. To his right sat his personal attorney, a seasoned and well-read guy named, Thomas J. Tyler. Next to the lawyer sat a silent business partner of Mr. Raymond, an elder guy named Emanuel Fleming. He was in the funeral and mortician business. To Mr. Raymond's left sat his sister named Cora. She served as his accountant and secretary. She was in her late 50s. Next to Cora was his wife of many years, Christine. And directly across the rectangular shaped table sat an investor by the name Joel Wynn. He was an arm's length away from Mr. Raymond.

Mr. Wynn was an astute late forties jovial white guy, that held a desire to purchase King of Dimez party haven, and transform it to a techno-rave type dance hall paradise for the up and vibrant diverse group of youth. To his right sat his attorney, Barry Harvey. To the left of Mr. Wynn sat his personal secretary and mistress of German descent named Rosalynn. And lastly, to her left sat his brother and business partner, Noel Wynn.

"Mitch! Please have a seat and let's get started, shall we," Mr. Raymond declared.

Mitch took a long look at every face present. Only a few he recognized.

"Now, what we have here Mitch, is the result of a decision that has been reached. And Mitch, my brother, in the next thirty days, a transition will occur. I—Raymond Eugene Stephens—no longer wishes to be involved in the clubbing industry at this point moving forward. I'm getting too old for this type of thing. And to cut through the chase so to directly reveal to you what this here is absolutely all about, in these words, I'm selling the club, bro. I have Mr. Wynn there present, to begin the process of buying me out. Pardon me on that. He's here to buy *us* out. We have the deeds, contracts, and all other relevant documents present, along with our attorneys to legalize the transactions that both sides seek to agree upon—"

"Excuse me! What did you just say!" Mitch cut him short to say. "Did I hear you correctly? Did you just say *sell* the club?" Mitch questioned.

'That's correct, Mitch. I intend to *sell* the club. Mr. Joel Wynn, is here to buy us out."

"Ray, pardon me for being a bit angry and confused. But for God's sake, why am I just now hearing about any of this? Why couldn't you and I have had a personal talk about what your designs are?" Mitch asked.

"Mitch, we've been friends for well over thirty years now, and in business in business for twenty-five of those. A few with the club, right?" Mr. Raymond asked.

"That sounds about right, Ray," Mitch replied.

"The bottom line is this, my guy. Ehere business begins, friendship ends! And What I have here, are the deeds to the land and the property of club King of Dimez night life entertainment social spot. Included are the contracts the both of us signed the moment we went into the business together and purchased the establishment," Mr. Raymond stated as he held separate documents in each hand waving them in the air for everyone to visualize.

"Hold up! Wait a minute there, Ray! Now I hear you out on your end of the spectrum, and I understand all you now desire to do with *your* share. But at no time will I ever agree to any of such, because I don't have no intentions to sell my stake in the club. I'm not selling out. I'm not signing over the rights, nor the deeds of the property to no one for no one. Not even for you, Ray! Now that's the bottom line," Mitch stated emphatically to Ray Ray Stephens as he looked on at him in disbelief in the way he'd talked to him.

"Mr. Collins, please allow me the opportunity to make you aware, that this deal is anywhere north of—"

The words of Mr. Wynn were immediately cut short by Mr. Raymond, from revealing the actual sum of the price to be paid for the purchase. He waved him quiet. Mr Raymond never discussed the numbers in the presence of anyone other than the person he dealt with directly. Once a deal had been completed, he revealed certain aspects to his accountant and attorney.

Mitch had inadvertently been injected into a situation where he was completely caught off guard. He didn't have his lawyer present, and he didn't have his personal copy of the contracts. Above all, the trust he held for Ray to ensure that all was well had been compromised severely.

"What about the family, Ray? The 'King of Dimez' family that works for us? How are they supposed to carry on? What about their dependency upon us to pay them? What about their loyalty, support, and commitment to the business and the brand we have built? What about *me*? My daughter that heads the bar area? Our security team? What am I to do if I sold out? I definitely don't intend to do so, but what do you think I'm to do, just take the money and blow it? What do you expect me to do? Waste my time?"

"What about it?" Mr. Raymond shrugged his shoulders in reply. "What about all you just mentioned and seem to hold a grave concern for? What about it?" He shrugged his shoulders again as he coldly responded.

"Are you for real, Ray? You got to be bullshitting me, right?"

"Look, Mitch, here is the deal. There will be a lot of money available for you to make here once the deal goes through, and—"

"What deal, Ray!" Mitch cut him off. "I'm not selling! I'm not agreeing to any of this. I want absolutely nothing to do with it, you hear me!" Mitch stated in a serious tone.

"Mitch, honestly, you can agree to this, or you can continue to be non-compliant and end up going through the process the hard way. Pick your poison. Nonetheless, the club is being sold and a deal will be finalized soon. The twelve percent stake that belongs to you will be allocated and deposited into an escrow account for you to retrieve later down the line."

"Twelve percent stake! Are you out of your frigging mind, Ray! You twenty-two percent short there, ain't you? I own thirty-four percent stake of the club and the brand," Mitch stated. "That twelve percent was the principal, NOT the sum total. What happened to all the profit I gained through the years?" Mitch questioned emphatically.

Before Mr. Raymond could reply, Mr. Wynn's lawyer chimed in. "Mr. Stephens, my client, Mr. Wynn here was under the impression that both parties would be in agreement on a deal?"

"The position you and your client have taken is understood, Mr. Harvey. And shall be accommodated on this day," Mr. Ray spoke up.

"Look!" Mitch yelled, attracting everyone's attention. "Let me make myself clear to all of you," he moved his finger from person to person as to exclude nobody from his wrath. "There won't be no fucking deal going down, if it requires my signature anywhere on a document! And to *you!*" he pointed his finger directly at Mr. Raymond. "I want to know about my fucking money from the profits directly reinvested back into the club! I don't know what you talking about with that twelve percent part. I'm *thirty-four* percent involved! That's where I intend to stay. Am I clear on that!"

"Is that a threat, Mitch?"

"That's whatever you take it to be, Ray. Straight like that. I'm glad to know that you've been very mendacious to me all these years. So much for family, huh. So much for the supreme parliament family, I suppose, right. It's all good. Now . . . if y'all would excuse me from this here meeting, I'll greatly appreciate it. I have more important business to attend to before I'm to appear at the other business tonight that I'm part owner of. And that's King of Dimez gentlemen club," stated the short, stocky, bearded behemoth in personality, ego, style, and assertion.

Mitch stood to his feet and was about to walk away when Mr. Raymond spoke again.

"Final offer, Mitch. It's on you, my guy."

Mitch looked him directly in the eyes. "No deal, Ray. No deal."

"Well then, fine. It was all on you. I tried. Just so you'll know, King of Dimez will be under new ownership and new management in the next few weeks. But in the meantime, the doors will be temporarily closed until further notice. Ain't no need to show up tonight unless Mr. Wynn here, intends to hire you to pressure wash the building and parking lot for him."

"We'll see about that then, won't we!" Mitch replied.

That motherfucking bitch-ass nigga got some nerve, don't he? How the fuck he gone make his mind up to sell the club outside of me knowing what the fuck was going on? This nigga didn't even care to ask me how I may feel or think or get my consent. He simply did what Ray wanted to do. Fuck me, huh! Just fuck us all together I guess, huh. And then, the thirty four percent that I'm in on the club, he just gone take twenty two percent of that from me, so he thought. I'll kill that nigga before I allow him to fuck me over out my money and my business! Everything about King of Dimez, I got something to do with it. I put my life into building that club up to where we got it, as it had served as a sure way for me to clean up my money from the ugly end. And not only that, what about all the dirt Ray and I had done together to make it thus far? What about the bodies we'd dropped to gain the upper hand in the game? I'm more than sure the nigga is going to cut me off from the supply line out of Mexico too. I just got to branch out and find my own connect. Shit is going to get tight for a while, but I'll make it. I need to get over to the club ASAP to get my valuables out of there.

Mitch thought about how treacherous Mr. Raymond had become as a tear rolled down his face. He'd been truly hurt by the underhanded move.

An idol of Mitch's had become a rival. An internal war was sparked, and somebody had to go.

Chapter 18

Mitch immediately made his way to the club so he could retrieve his money and other valuables tucked away there. This was all to no avail. When he arrived to the building, there were chains and huge Private Property—No Trespassing signs planted on the doors.

The truth of what compelled Mr. Raymond to part ways with Mitch was that, Mitch had sought to overthrow him in certain regards, by cutting side deals with a separate Mexican Cartel supplier called the Sinaloa Cartel. The backhanded move was brought to Raymond's attention by a high-ranking federal agent whom Mr. Raymond paid top dollars to. The Sinaloa Cartel was headed by the notorious and ruthless Señor El Chapo.

In Mr. Raymond's mind, Mitch would plot to kill him next, if he hadn't hurried and made his move to cut him loose. Also, Mitch began thinking that he ran King of Dimez. He was calling entirely too many shots and making too many decisions on his own. Mr. Raymond had had it with Mitch. Plain and simple.

Mr. Raymond had his sister pre-draft a message to send to the emails and text message telephone numbers of all the employees three days before the meeting. It read as follows:

ATTENTION-ATTENTION-ATTENTION! The alert went out to the employee group text.

This message applies to every employee that works or dances at King of Dimez Gentlemen Club. It is imperative that you immediately contact Mr. Raymond Stephens, to be made aware of the recent changes taking effect at 8:00 p.m. tonight regarding immediate changes. Please, DO NOT report to the establishment under no circumstances, for the doors are closed until further notice. More on the matter at a later date and time.

-Thank you.

Sincerely, Cora Stephens, Secretary to the owner.

At the conclusion of the deal, Mr. Raymond received $8,000,000 for the land and the buildings that rested on it. He was also slated to receive $4,000,000 for the K.O.D. logo and branding rights. He'd sold everything associated with the company. A move he appeared to not think twice about.

The security guard on hand of the property accosted Mitch when his presence was discovered.

"Sir! I'm going to have to ask you to leave immediately. You're trespassing," the security personnel stated.

"I'm trespassing! Motherfucker, who are you! I'm Mitch Collins, the co-owner of this here building! How the fuck you gone tell me to leave off the land I own!" Mitch replied vehemently.

"Sir, per order of a Mister Raymond Stephens and a Mister Joel Wynn, I have the authority to prevent anyone from entering onto the property," the tall, brawny, assertive, white, red head guard with a Marine crew cut retorted.

"You listen to me, you piece of shit!" Mitch aggressively uttered and pointed his finger in the guard's face as he walked up to him.

Crew cut pulled his pistol on Mitch and ordered him to the ground. He cuffed Mitch and called the police to come arrest him for trespassing and obstruction of officer. Mitch was livid with anger and vengeance. He was pissed off individual.

Chapter 19

Upon receiving the same group text that everyone at the club had gotten, Parlay reflected on the brief but pleasant tenure there and began to formulate a strategy on his future from there. It was best for him to expect nothing and strive to be self-sufficient. In other words, Parlay had to do what Parlay had to do, so to increase his chances of getting hired at other spots.

Miami and South Beach were both saturated with clubs, so finding work shouldn't have been a problem.

Later that evening, at Traci's, he broke the news to her about the club being sold.

"Everyone got laid off, sweetie. That included me too."

"You can't be for real, baby. What you plan to do now? I'm sure you got something in mind. However the situation turns out, you're good here at my place. We're good, baby. I promise you on that," she said.

She caressed him cheek and kissed on his jaw. Traci smiled from ear-to-ear as she ate from a bowl of fruit.

"Here, sweetie. You want some?" she seductively asked, offering to feed Parlay one of the strawberries dipped in whipped cream. He slithered out his tongue and licked the topping from the fruit, then lay back on the bed with his hands behind his head.

"Ooh, shit. Don't do it like that, baby. Ooh, please don't get me hot. You just turned me on. Damn, my pussy wet now. You just don't know what you've started, baby. It's on now," she stated as he got an instant erection beneath his Ralph Lauren Polo boxers. Parlay's manhood erected through the slit.

Traci dipped another strawberry and topped the tip of his manhood with the cream. With her tongue, she began to eat him raw, bobbing her head up and down on his gun. She was doing her best to make dude blast off shots of his love juice. She'd set the tempo and put him in the mood. It was on from that point forward.

The love birds fucked really good that night. Dude gave Traci the business, as he pained the pussy. That he certainly did do.

Chapter 20

Mitch posted bail after his arrest that day. He'd called Tisha to come pick him up. He related to her all that happened.

"Baby, I told you I had a gut feeling that that motherfucking nigga Ray, was up to no good! Look at the bullshit he put me through!"

"Yeah, I know right. Why didn't he have a conversation with you first daddy, before he ran off to do all of us like this?"

"Your guess is as good as mine, baby. That nigga has really done it this time! He caught me by total surprise, baby. By total surprise, you hear me. That nigga had the audacity to tell me, I'm only getting twelve percent of the money he sold the club for."

"Well, how much did he sell out for?"

"That's beside the point, baby! The nigga didn't have no business selling, period! I don't give a damn if he had been offered a *billion* bucks! I had no intent to sell the land and the building I put half the money down on. And then, I had almost $400,000 in money and jewelry in my safe at the club. That's what I was there to get. He and the buyer had the nerve to hire a security guard to watch over the property and keep trespassers away. I told that cracka,' I was one of the owners. He threw Ray and the buyer's name out there and that's when I lost it. That pecker-wood pulled his pistol on me, baby. The cotton-head cracka' drew down on your daddy and had me arrested."

"Ain't this a bitch! Have you tried to call him?"

"Nigga done changed the number of his personal line! I'll go by that nigga's house one day this week. That's what I'll do, baby. That nigga got to give me some answers. He got to tell Mitch something, you hear me! Nigga talking about he into politics now. What the fuck he thinking! Ray has truly lost it, baby. He really has."

"Well daddy, from a legal point of view, since y'all bought the land and the building together, and both of y'all names on the deeds, honestly, he can't sell without your signature, right?"

"Yeah, you right in a sense. But at the time we put up the money and got out the streets, me and Camille were together, and I had her put all I owned under her authority. When we broke up, the agreement was that we simply wouldn't have anything else to do with one another. I blessed her with $50,000 and let her go on about her way. I never took my share out of her name," Mitch related to his daughter. "A huge fuck up on my part."

Little to Mitch's knowledge, Raymond had long gotten Camille—the ex girlfriend—to sign off on the deeds, relinquishing authority from her and investing all of it in him. Mr. Raymond stole the beauty from under Mitch and carried on an affair, as Camille ended up being one of the main mistresses of Mr. Raymond. He sexed her quite frequently, and they went out on multiple dates in cities outside of Miami to keep Mitch out of the know. Raymond bought a home in Palm Beach and let Camille have it to live in. Any time he wanted to be with her, he would simply go to one of the homes he owned. He considered the house to her as a gift for the devious act she perpetrated against Mitch by signing over everything to Raymond, giving him full power to ownership of the land and the building.

Mitch was completely oblivious to the fact that Camille had taken all the problems that they experienced to his friend and business partner. Mr. Raymond, being the smooth talker and suave dude that he was, had been able to serenade her with his speech and assuage her emotionally with care and affection.

The things that Mitch had been terrible at doing or failed to perform at all, Camille had been able to receive through the other, for many practical reasons. She'd fallen in love with Ray and had not the slightest care or concern for the dangerous games that she played. Camille had gone so far as to give RayRay almost a million dollars in cash and other highly expensive items to him that once belonged to Mitch, like paintings, glass china pieces, jewelry, and silverware. Exactly what happened was, she feigned innocence and claimed that someone had broken into the house. But in all actuality, Camille had set up the entire thing, by providing her hired burglars with a set of keys to the home and the pass-codes to deactivate the alarms while she and Mitch were away on vacation in his family's native Haiti and the D.R. When they returned, the job had been thoroughly completed, as the thieves were able to take their time in doing so.

Mr. Raymond and Camille were still very intimate to the present day, as she continued to occupy the home that he'd put her in. She had no contact with Mitch since they'd split, and he had no knowledge of her whereabouts.

The conversation between Mitch and his daughter continued.

"So, in other words, daddy, your portion of the land and the club, is still under Camille's name?" Tisha inquired.

"That's correct, baby."

"Well, have you tried to contact her?"

"Ray just now hitting me with the bullshit, baby. Now, I definitely got to get in contact with her before he does, if I can locate her. Last I knew, she moved to Seattle, Washington where she has family. But I figure it shouldn't be too hard to get in touch with her. She still loves me, and I still love her, you know," Mitch stated.

My daddy has really lost his damn mind! Tisha thought what she couldn't say openly of her father.

"Just please keep control of your anger and don't do anything that'll get you in trouble, daddy," Tisha said to her father.

"I'll make sure to try and keep that in mind," Mitch replied.

——

One week later . . .

Yolanda contacted the Love Dolls Lounge on 79th street in an effort to ink a deal.

Love Dolls was considered the second hottest strip club in the city behind K.O.D., and had gained the number one spot by default when Mr. Raymond cashed in. Mr. Raymond's intentions for her were genuine, being that she'd brought him a lot of money and popularity, with her eye for identifying talent.

In the same vein, he held an infatuation for Yolanda that bordered on that of a stalker. Mr. Raymond hated being denied for anything, especially the attention of a female. Not to mention the fact that he barely knew Yolanda personally. His entire objective was to have his way with her, in the manner he saw fit. But Yolanda wasn't having it. Not from him. Not from Big Mix. Not from Parlay. Not from any of those thirsty dudes whom drooled from the mouth and yearned for her lustfully. However, Mr. Raymond failed to get to the point. It would be a costly ordeal for him at some point or another, if he continued to not take heed of what was truly brewing just below the surface of things. His focus was detoured.

On the flip-side, Big Mix was probably the most obsessed with her, and his nose was wide open in the hopes of smelling the fragrance of what her rose garden had to offer. Mix had always spewed his guts on what he knew regarding the private life, the scandals, the affairs, the business dealings, the gains, the losses, and all else Mr. Raymond. He operated as personal bodyguard and driver, so he knew a lot. He'd blabbered his life away to Yolanda. And all she had to do, was spend a little time with him, allow him a kiss every now and again, and let him masturbate off her while she danced in one of her outfits. Big Mix equipped her with valuable Intel. Even against himself. He was in for a huge surprise.

—

Parlay managed to apply a small business license. He eventually was granted one, and he opened and operate a vehicle detail shop. His objective was to withdraw some of the funds from his mother's bank account and finance a building. This became a foreseeable plan for a prosperous future.

He contacted his cousin Vick, and asked that he stop by the house, so he could give him the rundown on all things vehicle detailing, being that Vick specialized in such area, as he'd previously held a job at a BMW dealership. The two planned to take a stroll through the city and do a little parking lot pimping at the clubs. Parlay felt the need to put his macking skills to the test so to see if or not he still had it. Once upon a time, he could talk a bitch or two clean out of their panties and end up getting the pussy the same day.

Vick had something really important to tell Parlay, and it couldn't wait. He knew Parlay would definitely want to hear all he had to say about this particular subject.

"Nigga, you ain't going to believe who the fuck I came across the other day while leaving Burger King!" Vick exclaimed.

"Who that, cuz?"

"It was that fuck-nigga, Calvin Prescott! I wanted to pull my pistol out and pop that pussy-ass nigga right there on the spot! I started to call you, but I didn't want you to get into no more trouble. He didn't notice me though."

"I thought that nigga moved to Fort Myers or Tallahassee, or some other place?"

"Yeah, he did. But he back now. Most likely, because he broke and down on his luck," Vick said.

"It's all good, cuz. That snitch-ass nigga going to get what's coming to him. I promise you on that. Rather by me or someone else. He's due a severe punishment."

"But anyway, my nigga, lets hit the club. I wanna check out a few bitches."

Shortly thereafter, Vick and Parlay were vibing in one of his favorite bar spots, as the crowd did their thing on the dance floor. The two strutted over to the pool table section to shoot a few rounds. Vick was a semi pool sharp on the low. He had excellent form and focus. He beat the shit out of Parlay for those two games they played. Parlay couldn't fuck with that nigga on no level. Vick was simply too good.

—

Afterwards, the two cousins headed to the bar for a few drinks. Suddenly, out of nowhere, Parlay was approached by this female named Tina Daniels whom he used to date long before his arrest. He had a nickname for her. It was "Terrific Tina," due to the magnificent skills she had at doing one specific thing very well

"Hey, Parlay! How you been, sweetie? Long time, no see. With your handsome self."

She was always one of his best cut-buddies, and blew his mother fucking brains out with passion and dedication each and every time she gave the nigga a good dick suck. That bitch had perfected the art and craft of deep-throat and tea-

139

bagging. This was how she'd personally earn the nickname he laid upon her.

"Well, hello there, Tina. How are you, Miss Thang? Damn right, it's been a long time. And I'm glad to see you too"

"So, what girl was lucky enough to catch you when you got free? I'd heard you'd went away for a time being."

"I'm not involved in a committed relationship per se. But I do have a friend I kick it with for the sake of having a somebody, you feel me." He didn't want to blow any opportunity there was for them to possibly get busy.

His manhood began to tingle and throb from the sensation of Tina brushing up against him and whispering in his ear throughout the conversation they had. Her breath was fresh and smelled of peppermint, even though she sipped on a bottle of Budweiser beer, a "pony" (7 oz. bottle). Parlay knew for sure without a doubt that before long while the both of them was engaged in a semi deep conversation, Tina was bound to say something leaning towards them hooking up at some point. They'd always shared great chemistry. Never a dull moment between them.

Tina produced a pretty smile as she must had relished in a thought from their past as she chomped down on the gum she chewed. Then, she popped one on him.

"Parlay. You still got that dope dick on you, my nigga?" He smiled in amazement, because he knew it was coming.

"And you got to know I do, sweetheart. It may be even better now, since I've been on reserve for seventeen years. Now, let me ask you something, since we popping these type of questions."

"What's that, sweetie?"

"You still got that fire-ass head on you?" he let out as he'd taken a good look at those juicy lips of hers.

"Ain't lost a beat or a battle since a month of Sundays, playboy," she said very confidently, and popped her lips in a sassy-like manner.

"Is that right, boo! Well, check this out. I'm available if you are?" he made known to her.

"What took you so long to mention that to me? Let's get to the money," Tina stated and pointed in the direction of the restrooms with her handheld purse clutched in her palm.

"Yo, cuz, I'll be back shortly," Parlay leaned in and said to Vick, as Tina grabbed him by the hand and lead the way.

This bitch was so for real and so gangsta about handling her business. Raunchy too, might it be added. She had the nerve to wink at Vick as to silently indicate to him that she was going to "eat Parlay alive." Parlay definitely liked that shit. It really geek him to the max.

The two went inside the women restroom area and immediately occupied a stall. As they began kissing, he unbuckled his pants. They wasted no more time with the talking. All he had to do was grab the top of the stall and hold on for dear life. She whipped out his pipe for him and took him into her mouth. It didn't take long for him to reach erection. He was already near the point to begin with. Tina gobbled down on dude aggressively. She then bobbed back and forth, doing her best to ensure that she pleased the King. That nasty-ass bitch had always brought out the beast in Parlay. He was head over hills for her oral sex performance.

Tina drooled a thick coat of spit on the dick and got extra sloppy with it. *Damn, it feels so good! This bitch still got the best head in all Miami! Nah, fuck that! She got the best head in all the sunshine state period!* he thought to himself.

Her grip was extra tight around his shaft, as she jerked him off and bobbed her head simultaneously, trying to bring him to the top.

"Ahhh, yeah, Tina! just like that, girl. You still the truth, ain't you," he said to her. His compliment gave an added boost of confidence, as the bitch turned into a superstar head doctor.

"I'm about to blow a load, girl," he let her know.

Right after, he let go all of himself, as he blasted full force in her mouth. Dude shot off four thick streaks of potent elixir. She swallowed every drop. Tina sucked him up and licked clean all that was left. She then pulled out a two-ounce bottle of Listerine and rinsed her mouth. Then she popped a piece of gum in and began to chomp more.

"You good now, ain't you?" she asked teasingly. "That boy done got straight," she teased more.

"And you know it," Parlay responded happy-like. "Tina, you still the truth, girl," he added as they locked eyes.

"You think so? Just wait until we sho' nuff get to the money at some point soon," she stated.

"That's a bet. Here's my number. Get at me when you feel like it," he said as she locked his number in her contacts.

"Parlay, you already know anytime we hook up, it's all on me, so don't worry, we're good. I owe you anyway, for the times that you accepted me and took good care of me. That was my welcome home gift to you. Besides, I like the way you taste." Tina smiled behind her words.

"Well thank you. And I definitely appreciate the gift," he replied with a smile.

They kissed once more and left the restroom.

———

Parlay got Vick's attention and they got up out of there, now headed to post up in the parking lot of a different club.

Cruising from one destination to the next, Vick got serious-toned and initiated a much desired conversation.

"Cuz, what you intend to do now since the club thing over with?" he asked.

"Shit, cuz, I don't know yet, my nigga. I ain't fully made my mind up. I do have my small business license, and I wanted to do something with that. I would like to try my hand at starting a small business or something to that effect. Detailing vehicles maybe," he replied to the inquiry.

"Oh, yeah, that sound straight too. I don't know if you ready to hear this yet, but if you're interested, shit really been lovely on my end along through the 'Iron Pipeline.' I've gotten back into the business since you been away. This happened about five years ago. It only required me to dibble-and-dabble a few times throughout the month. That's about it. Nothing too major. It pays off well too, cuz. Like, for real it does."

Gun trafficking was the very offense that caused Parlay to be tucked away in federal prison. However, that was the hustle he knew best. It allowed him the opportunity to eat well.

"Cuz, you say it's lovely, right? But just how lovely is it?" he inquired.

"Real lovely. I'm talking about, anywhere from $500 to $2,000 for one brand new Glock. And those A-R's will definitely have you filthy rich in short order," Vick replied.

The promise Parlay made to his mother had ran through his mind,

Momma I promise you that I won't be getting my behind locked up no more and causing you all of that stress and depression I had as my time was served out.

He rapidly weighed the options. Vick spoke in depth to entice him to join the team. "Yeah, Parlay, you already know I'm a huge NRA guy that strongly believe in the second Amendment. I was sure to maintain being felony free for a reason, fam. I'm tied in with a few money hungry white boys in Georgia, Alabama, Tennessee, and Mississippi, who all own gun shops and have everything you can think of available, from a twenty-two derringer, to a 50-caliber rifle with the kick stand on it. I also got street niggaz locked in who perform night raids on vulnerable gun and pawn shops in these southern states. I get forty percent of all I sell from those takes. The biggest and most committed customers are those Latin motherfuckers up north in New York, Jersey, and Philly. You got some major street teams up the way also, that need protection and enforcement over their enterprises and products, especially in DC, Camden, Trenton, and *'Bodymore.'* They want all we got to offer," Vick related. "Just think about it, my nigga. I'm here," he lastly stated on the subject.

Parlay internalized all Vick related, and allowed it to rest on his mind. Truth be told, he did itch to get back with the program. Indeed, the money to be made was more than enough to make him say, *fuck it,* I'm in! That was due to Vick making it known that he was paid in various ways, and at times by narcotics such as heroin, ice, bricks of cocaine, opiates, etc. He accepted payment however it came.

Parlay remembered a time before when the both of them had a conversation while he was locked up and Vick related he took a payment from a guy named "Fat Aaron" up in the "Big Apple" of eight game breed pitbull puppies. Ain't that a bitch! Vick had also gotten into the dog fighting area as well. He developed a love and sincere appreciation for pit-bulls. Fat Aaron was from out of Harlem New York. If I was not mistaken, I believe I'd read something about that dude in a book by the highly respected and legendary hood novelist named Khalil. The book was titled *Road Dogs.*

But to be totally honest, I had already made my mind up long before the conversation with Vick.

Chapter 21

Since the sell of the club, Parlay had not heard anything from Mr. Raymond or Mitch. He'd began to wonder, what provoked Mr. Raymond to sell the club? He loved that spot, as his progress was steady. And not only that, he adored the ladies and the attention received from them. What could have brought about such a sudden change in focus?

His mind was vexed on getting to the bottom of the situation, and so, he utized a phone number he had. Parlay texted Tisha first, to know if or not she was free to talk. She was. Tisha told him to call. And that he did.

"Hello! Tisha here," she answered.

"Hey! Tisha. How are you, my girl?"

"I'm doing well. My guy. How you been, baby?" she responded with so much energy and excitement.

"I've been maintaining the struggle, sweetie. I've been maintaining the struggle. That's what I've been doing. The reason I called is because, I'm trying to understand what the hell happened?"

"It's a lot, Melvin. A lot, I tell you. The bottom line is that, Mr. Raymond sneaky ass, did some low down and shady shit to my father, Melvin!"

"I thought everything was going good between those two?"

"Everything *was* going good. But apparently, Ray decided he wanted to step into the world of politics and needed to maintain a clean reputation for public favor."

"Oh! That's what the deal is, huh? Mr. Raymond trying to be a public servant. But I thought if he had a co-partner, a co-owner of land and property, it would require the signature of them both before any sell could go on?" he stated. Actually digging to know more.

"Yes, you're right on that. Ray had set up this meeting between him and the buyer who is some rich white guy, and invited my father at the eleventh hour to be in on it. My dad said that he arrived at the meeting, looking for it to be him, Ray, and maybe one to two other people from the K.O.D. Family to eat a meal or celebrate some type of way. And what does he get surprised with? It's Ray, his lawyer, his wife, and a few others on his side of the table looking to finalize a deal. And across from them, you got the buyer, his lawyer, and others on this team. Ray completely blind-sided my father with the move he made. Took him off guard. He had not been prepared for that. Not in the least," Tisha related.

"Well how did a deal go through without your dad's signature?" Parlay further inquired.

"Ray had done all he could in his efforts to try and persuade my father to sign off on the deeds, but my father refused, because he had no intent to sell out. And, he wanted to remain in the stable position he owned as a COO of the club. I don't know if I should be telling you this or not, but at the time my dad and Ray bought the club, my dad was a married man, and he had a multitude of different things going on from a street level and perspective. Putting the establishment in his own name, wouldn't have been a smart thing to do. He put everything in his wife's name, my stepmother," Tisha revealed.

"Oh, I see now. So, Mr. Raymond never got the deal finalized, did he?" he asked.

"That is the hope my dad clings dear to. The problem is, my dad can't locate his wife since they separated. He don't know where she is so he can sign the deed out of her name and put it under my authority."

146

"Why didn't he do that to begin with?"

"Because I was involved with a street dude myself that was tied to my dad on an underworld level. He's the father of my kids, and that wouldn't have been good for business either. He didn't want me scrutinized by the watchful eyes of the feds as they investigated Sekou. My stepmother had a clean profile than me. She also was a real-estate agent, so that just made better sense," she said.

"I'm understanding."

"But get this too, Melvin. I had to bail my dad out of jail the same day of that so-called meeting."

"Why? What happened?"

"That snake-ass nigga Ray, had got with the buyer, and they hired a security guard to patrol the property. My dad went to the club to be made aware of the full extent of the sale and to also get his belongings. He had money, jewelry, and other valuables in a safe in his office. He attempted to use his key, but the doors had thick chains and locks to prevent access. Then he gets into a rough argument with the guard, and the white boy drew down on daddy, cuffed him, and called the cops. Melvin, I ain't never seen my daddy more pissed than he was that day! He still hot to this day. Somebody is going to get seriously hurt. I just don't want to see my father in any trouble," Tisha stated.

"Everything's going to be alright. Maybe he and Mr. Ray will be able to work things out for the better," Parlay said encouragingly.

"I don't think so, Melvin. I believe it's too far out of hand now. But anyway, on another note. You had a bitch feeling like she had played herself or something, being that it took you so long to call back. Nonetheless, you did call," she said.

"Tisha, now you should already have a good idea of how I operate. I'm a very patient and calculated fella, that loves to take my time in doing things. If there's one thing prison taught me, that was how to have discipline. Patience plays a part too. But discipline is the main key to unlock any doors to mastery," Parlay stated to her.

"Well, did you call to talk to me, or did you call to be nosy about my father?" Tisha asked sassy-like.

"I called because I was concerned. I'm no longer employed, and your dad did play a vital role in me getting hired. I was wondering if you could ask him to allow you to provide me his number so I can call? I wouldn't mind talking to him to find out what the next move might be, and if he would like to have me on board? But to be honest, I had you on my mind as well." He lied to get her to talk more.

"Awe, that's so sweet and thoughtful of you. I miss seeing that handsome facebof yours. And I definitely miss that nice-ass body of yours."

"Oh, you do?"

"You damn right, I do."

"I hope that damn Yolanda or no other chick ain't locked you down and made you commit before I have the chance to show you how I'm able to please a man," she said in a modest way to reveal parts of her inner-self and the crush she had for him.

Damn! What beef she got against Yolanda? Why would she mention her name? Parlay thought to himself.

"Now, if that was the case, if I were involved with someone, I sure as hell wouldn't disrespect them no type of way by having an extensive conversation with another woman. I'll have the same level of respect I would want them to have for me," he stated.

"That sounds about right. That definitely sounds about right. But to answer your question about my dad, I will certainly set it up for you and him to have a phone conversation or possibly meet up and discuss a few things. He's got plans to open up a spot of his very own sometime soon. He mentioned something about the security team and specifically mentioned you by name. No need to worry, it wasn't anything bad. I was sure to put in a good word for you already. This will be after we go out on our first date. And don't be surprised if you get a call asking if you would be interested in leading the next team of bouncers for the spot the Collins family will exclusively own and fully operate," she stated.

"That would be nice," Parlay replied pleasantly.

"Melvin, I want to be honest with you, okay."

"I wouldn't want it no other way, sweetheart."

"It's no secret as you already know. I like you in a major way, and I wouldn't mind the two of us getting to know each other or possibly being together on a deeper level. I've had a serious crush on you since the day I had the pleasure to lay eyes on you. I was turned on like never before. I've never felt this way about a man at no point in my life. It's becoming an uncontrollable infatuation. For lack of better terms, I'm a hopeless romantic, Melvin. I would like to reveal more of myself to you some day, if only you would let me and accept me," she stated.

Damn baby-girl! This a little too much for a nigga right now, he thought to himself but dared against letting her in on all he concealed.

"Tisha, we got time for that. I promise you we do. We'll see how things go."

"Are you busy this weekend?" she asked.

"I might not be. What's up?"

"I was thinking maybe, we could go out on a date or something, being that we had such a good time talking at the club. We could do the Palm Beach experience or something if you like?"

Parlay took a long pause before he was to give her an answer. It was a must that he thought his way through before committing. He had to come up with something to tell Traci to excuse his absence, if he decided to take Tisha up on her offer. She had to work all weekend anyway. A sixteen hour day and a twelve hour day. So it wasn't like Traci would miss him. Clearly, she wouldn't. And such outing with Tisha, would afford him the perfect opportunity to situate himself deeper into her life. This was what she wanted after all, and he didn't mind delivering. How could he lose if she has already chosen? And besides, the date was all on her, reservations and the whole nine.

"Yeah, I'll go. We can do that. I really enjoyed a previous trip there before, and it's worth a second visit," he said in agreement.

"Good. I'll be sure to take care of the reservations and book events we'll be attending. But on the meeting with my dad, I'll do anything and everything necessary to help you make your rise to power through him. I'm going to definitely take care of things for you. Even if it boils down to me strongly voicing my opinion for you and co-signing for on a top position with my father. Don't worry, I got you covered, baby," Tisha stated.

"Well, I thank you, and I can't wait to see you this weekend. I know you love the video-chat thing, but just give me some time to get into that. I'm sorry, I got an 'old-school' bone in my body. We didn't have all this back then. But I'll get at you Friday, okay."

"Okay, Melvin. And you take care for me, sweetie."

"Likewise," he concluded.

Following the conversation he'd held with Tisha, he deeply contemplated over a few possible things related to the potential future that awaited him as a prominent security guard in the clubbing business, or either with a high profile figure. He had to admit, to himself, he'd taken a liking to the profession of security, and sought to learn as much as possible to build a team of his own to contract services to various other enterprises instead of being limited to clubs.

Parlay's thoughts reverted to the rift between the two former owners of King of Dimez. Tisha revealed much that he had no knowledge of. He never thought for once that Mr. Raymond had a cutthroat bone in his body. It had always appeared that he and Mitch were close and tight-knit as two friends and business partners should be. They seemed like brothers, or more like the biblical story of Cain and Abel, One crossed the other, then eventually killed him. Who was to say what the outcome of the former club bosses' situation would turn out to be? Only time would tell. But Tisha did state that Mr. Ray was going into politics, and needed a cleaner image for public favor. So, hey, that's what aspiring politicians have to do in that particular world, clean up their image, so to not suffer damaging attacks from rivals.

But on another note, Tisha clearly revealed that she was head over hills for him. The moment she wasted no time to pass him her phone number, he'd taken heed of the fact. Parlay liked the attention she provided, but he failed to understand the dislike she held towards Yolanda. Was it jealousy maybe? Or even a dose of envy perhaps? Whatever the case may be, it was definitely something there. But nonetheless, he owed a lot to Yolanda. If Tisha knew that much, it was a must to maintain a respectable rapport in that regard. Besides, he took a liking to her and her gorgeous features, along with her sexy body. She was nice.

Parlay's infatuation and lust for Yolanda had been tamed and placed under control for all the wise reasons. He felt that they would make out better as business partners and friends, over any superficial thought or desire to have one another. Business and pleasure could not co-exist at any one time between an attractive man and woman if not a married couple, as Yolanda had long preached down this line. Tisha may have had the ups on Yolanda in that regard. However, on the other hand, if she wanted to take it further and allow an intimate dealing to overrule the business and friendship part, undoubtedly, Parlay would be compelled to find a way to reap the benefits that came along with Tisha, and hold on to Yolanda behind the scenes. It would be a balancing act one could utilize to great effect. If anything, he knew he could be the one to pull it off between the divide of those two princesses that were on their rise to power one way or another.

As he continued to think of Yolanda, his mind see-sawed from subject to subject in mental effort to know how to take her. On the real, he didn't know a fucking thing about her. He had no knowledge of where she lived. He didn't know anything about her family, or her up-bringing. Nor did he know if Yolanda was in fact of a male or a female gender. He didn't know if "she" had a pussy or a dick. "She" could've been a transsexual for all he knew. In today's society, you just never could tell. He did feel good about her, but the question remained, *was everything all good with her?* He truly didn't know. Hopefully, her truth would be revealed some day, if in fact she had something to hide or not.

Chapter 22

Mr. Raymond contacted his long time buddy Emanuel, and had him come over to the house for the two of them to have a much needed conversation. Mr. Raymond immediately began talking once the elder of them arrived.

"Emanuel, I'm so glad you could make it. I sent Christine and Erin off to go shopping for the weekend up in New York, to give us enough time to talk business and to sell off everything we've got left, count up all the cash we have on hand, and basically do a thorough clean-up of all we got going on in the underworld. I wanted to do it long before I make my official announcement to join the Mayoral race as a candidate.

"I understand you, Ray. I'm here, buddy. Ol' Emanuel may be seventy-one going on thirty, but I still got your back. Lord knows I only wished that your brother, my best friend Phillip, was still living to celebrate the success we have experienced, and the transition we about to make. I swear I do, Ray," Emanuel stated with teary eyes of the fond thoughts and mourning of Mr. Raymond's brother that was believed to have passed away in 1993.

Phillip was the eldest of four boys. He died from internal bleeding and a collapsed lung following a car accident that occurred as he was on his way back to Miami from Tennessee on Interstate 75—the Florida Turnpike—near Orlando. He'd been badly injured but took no heed to the fact as he did the unthinkable, by checking himself out of the hospital half-treated. That was following him regaining consciousness due to the paranoia and fear he had at the thought of hired hit-men of rivals being ordered to take him out, or the Feds running down on him to lock him away forever.

Phillip and Emanuel had been buddies since they were in third grade, and also ripped, roamed, and dwelt in the streets of Miami, committing petty crimes and being the hoodlums that underprivileged teenagers are stereotyped to be. The two were closer as friends than Phillip were to his very own biological brothers.

Phillip acquired his money, reputation in the hood, and legendary status following his release from federal prison back in the early 80's. He and two other comrades had robbed a bank in Miami for a sum total of $4.5 million dollars. Emanuel was excluded from the robbery crew, due to him being away out of town following a death in the family. All three individuals involved in the caper were tracked down and arrested by the FBI. This was three weeks after the heist. However, they were smart enough to stash their take and share of the proceeds that the bank provided.

While in the pen, Phillip linked up and connected with one of the top commanding suppliers from the original "Cocaine Cowboys," and also, with a drug lord from the Dominican Republic. Both of the narcotic czars provided him with a direct line to their people to keep Phillip equipped with some of the best and purest product around. He played the hand well he'd been dealt, and banked on the money he had put away to afford him a good start at the point of his eventual release.

Once freed, after eight years, he returned to the streets he knew best and took over a strip of turf along the infamous and notorious 15th Avenue in Liberty City. Phillip had kilos of cocaine now laid out all over the hood like cow shit dotted in an open pasture. He became the "*Man*" and took good care of the people that resided in his neighborhood where he reigned as *"chief."*

Phillip owed Emanuel a great debt of gratitude for his loyalty and staying down with him as a friend throughout his bid. Emanuel managed to straighten out his own life during the time his friend was away. He was initiated as a Free-Mason and joined a lodge under the charter of the Prince Hall line and order. As a reward for his loyalty, Phillip put up the money for Emanuel to acquire a license as a Mortician through the lodge. The land to establish the cemeteries was purchased by Phillip as well, as he believed in Emanuel greatly, along with the vision he possessed. A bond and partnership was cemented for Phillip to supply the narcotics and the proceeds while Emanuel held the duty to dig the graves to hide the cocaine and the money that was produced abundantly.

Phillip was believed to be dead two weeks after he checked himself out of the hospital. It was never confirmed if or not, the decomposed body that was recovered from his home was in fact his. Phillip had a home in Miami lakes, which was located on the North part of the city, and ordered that the place be equipped with extra security measures that included a 2,000 pound steel door that led to the master bedroom. He had holed himself up in the room seeking to fully recover and also be provided the much needed time to himself that he so badly desired without his wife, daughter, nor bodyguard. Phillip sent her and their eight year old daughter off on an elaborate shopping spree that was to last a week in New York City, as Vanessa befriended the sister of one of his Dominican partners and drug suppliers. The wife Vanessa, spoke fluent Spanish, as she was Venezuelan, and that afforded her to bond and get along well with the Dominican wife of Phillip's friend and supplier, a Dinelo Blandan.

Phillip supposedly passed away while Vanessa was up north shopping and touring the "Big Apple." As mentioned, he was home alone, and supposedly "died" alone, being that no one was there to call paramedics or to resuscitate him at the moment of being unresponsive. He left behind 500 kilos of cocaine, $15 million in cash and gold ingots, and two million in land and property deeds, including those for the funeral parlors and cemeteries he and Emanuel co-owned that only Emanuel had access to. Emanuel had direct instructions that if Phillip should die, he was to team up exclusively with RayRay, and thoroughly teach him the game as they knew it. That was exactly what Emanuel had done. He'd joined forces with Ray and kept the movement going, introducing him to the connects, the pipeline, and the team, so to prosper and be a profitable businessman.

It was highly suspected that Phillip had faked his death and fled the country in route to Venezuela to duck indictments and possibly the dreaded electric chair behind all the people whom had been killed on his orders. Those was the accusations throughout his "deadly reign."

The theory was that, he and Emanuel orchestrated the entire thing by purposely planting a body from the funeral home inside his bedroom. Supposedly, the corpse was the same height and weight as him behind the 2,000 pound steel door that was smelled by the wife due to decomposition and later discovered for her to call authorities.

The Feds appeared at the funeral ten deep, as people from all walks of life showed up to pay their last respects. The FBI had taped the parts of the service, took photos, and scrutinized the entire occasion. They even went so far as to tap on the casket to see if it was hollow or not, speculating that a body may not be inside. It was a closed-casket burial. Might it also be mentioned that Phillip's wife, Vanessa, was no longer sighted around shortly after the funeral. Her mysterious disappearance contributed to the suspicion of the federal government that their target had pulled a Harry Houdini on them, due to Miss Vanessa seemingly falling off the face of the earth. Long story short, that was how the strong acquaintance between Mr. Raymond and Emanuel was forged. They were partners for life.

"You got to excuse me with this filthy laundry room down here in this basement, Emanuel. This the best and the safest spot we have right now to truly talk, until the "Ground Hog Hotel" gets fully renovated and properly equipped. We don't want to fuck around and suffocate down there in that motherfucker, do we?" Mr. Raymond stated as he and Emanuel shared a laugh at the comment.

The both of them had a near death experience together behind an air tunnel being clogged to the safe haven they had built.

The "Ground Hog Hotel," was an underground bunker that was thirteen feet below the surface in a cemetery on 43rd street and 32nd Ave, NW in the "Sub" or Brownsville section of Miami. It was only a football field length down from a playground on the same street. The entrance to the "Hotel" was through the front gate to a mausoleum and an elevated tombstone that had a hydraulic lift to it and opened on one side like a door that was flat. There was exactly eight steps down the staircase that led to a 13 X 13 foot chamber, about the size of a mini boxing ring buried underground. It was equipped with one over-head light that was powered by a line pole near the street and ran underneath to the hidden stash house. There was also a small table with two money machines to count cash that was temporarily placed there, along with several kilos of supply until transport was necessary or laundering was called for. That was the original locale. The newly built haven was located in the cemetery on 135th Street in Opalocka.

"Emanuel, I need for you to pull up all the work we got left to get rid of. What all need to be inventoried?" Mr. Raymond questioned.

Emanuel, always the one to keep with true old school beliefs, spoke in coded language in the event that the house had been bugged by the feds.

"If they wanted you, there ain't no length that they wouldn't go to get you, Ray. Just keep that in mind before you speak so loosely. But, in the land down under, we got forty pounds of 'Wrong Turn,'" that was code for meth/Ice), "and thirty-five thousand pills of each brand of "Opp." This was code for opiates. "Oh yeah, since we on the subject, I wanted to mention to you something I read in the Wallstreet Journal, not long ago," Emanuel stated.

"What's that?" Mr. Raymond inquired.

"There was an ad titled 'Firm stops promoting OxyContin to doctors,' and it said Purdue's aggressive. Excuse me, let me get it right. It said, many public health officials have said that Purdue's aggressive marketing of OxyContin after the launch of the drug in nineteen ninety-six, helped encourage lax prescribing and widespread addiction that many people progressed from to heroin and other illicit drugs. More than 30,000 . . . excuse me again, more than 300,000 Americans have died from opioid overdoses since late nineteen nineties. It also added that in 2004, Purdue, the pharmaceutical company that produces OxyContin, and three of its executives, pleaded guilty in federal court to criminal charges of misleading the public about the addictive qualities of OxyContin. Now that's from the Wallstreet Journal," Emanuel stated.

"Ain't that a bitch," Mr. Raymond responded to the news Emanuel had provided.

"Damn sho' is, ain't it now?" replied the mortician slash dope and narcotics pusher.

"So, what family you got everything located that's not in the hotel?" Mr. Raymond asked. By that he meant what alphabetical section of the cemetery was the material located.

"Well, our new president's last name's Trump, so I figured I'll let them hold everything down for us on a presidential level. The 'T' family, Don Jr, Eric, Ivanka,

Barron, and the wife," Emanuel stated four separate graves sites that held four different products.

With a smile and a chuckle behind Emanuel's humor, Mr. Raymond replied, "Good. Call a family meeting for the Trumps."

Emanuel knew that this meant to exhume everything.

"Send them all the way to Russia. With love if you have to," Mr. Ray instructed. Emanuel didn't have to ask because it was evident that he meant for him to sell everything as fast as possible.

"Make it cold as ice and heavy snow, just like the socialist nation that Russia is."

Nodding, Emanuel already was smart enough not to leave anything for the feds and turn the trail cold.

"No evidence, no case long before the dossier documents gets unsealed and revealed." He was speaking of the potential federal indictments.

My Raymond lowered his voice to a whisper and asked, "How many of them pills you say left again?"

"There is thirty-five thousand each. You got OxyContin, subsys, Nucynta, Duragesic, and Tramadol. Remember the last drop we received? There was one million each. Now we down to the number I just gave you. That ain't bad, is it?" Emanuel replied.

"No sir, it ain't. I got a few well established and high rolling white guys up in West Virginia, Tennessee, and Kentucky, that's been pretty consistent and hungry for them all. We should be able to cover the order, you know. Once we get rid of everything, I've got to go meet Senor in his country and take my nephew along to be introduced. We going to keep the money rolling in, but Phil Jr, is going to be the new face of the enterprise now, as you and I fade to black from this perspective and create or invest into Fortune 500 companies or other businesses to make the money right," Mr. Raymond stated.

"What about the Mitch situation," Emanuel inquired?

"He's got his portion of the last supply. We made sure he got his 250,000 of each pill and he got his eighty pounds of 'Wrong Turn.' At the meeting, I tried to get him to sign off on the deeds, but he refused. No need to worry about any of that. I have taken care of all the legal discrepancies that was subject to arise. And that nigga's twelve percent, I deposited into an Escrow for him to retrieve whenever. I had my lawyer take care of everything and ensured I couldn't be sued. Also, Senor knows he's no longer on board and all the reasons why. He asked if I want my problems to be gone forever. I told him it was no need. It wasn't that serious. But Mitch, is out the way, to answer your question. How soon can you make this happen?" Mr. Raymond asked.

The two continued to talk a little while longer.

———

Emanuel departed Mr. Raymond's home in Coconut Grove en route to take care of the business he was assigned to do. Mr. Raymond, on the other hand, took a seat behind the screen of his computer and continued with his research regarding municipal politics and principalities so to refine himself on his abilities and intellectual capabilities to lead the culturally diverse city of Miami. His preparation and registry had been very intense as Mr. Raymond already declared himself the "unofficial Mayor" of Miami. He catered to the needy by invoking philanthropic principles on every major holiday and many occasions in between since the day he draped himself dapper, stood before the body-length mirror, and held a lengthy one on one conversation with himself serious minded as he declared, "I am somebody! I'm the Mayor of Miami. And I'm the people's champ. So help me God, I am!"

Mr. Raymond may had been a bit zealous with his exaggerations or even delusional in a sense, but nonetheless, supremely confident, and intent on being a potentially great black politician someday. Indeed, like Scarface, he felt "The World Was His." Would his predictions become a reality, or were they simply a figment of his imagination?

Mr. Raymond then pulled out his cell phone and opened the contacts app. He texted Big Mix and told him to call ASAP. Mix followed the orders of his boss and replied two minutes later.

"Mix, what's good, my guy! Everything kosher on your end?" Mr. Raymond answered upon notice of the number.

"Of course, it is. What's on your mind, Mr. Ray?" Mix asked.

"Not too much. I need you to be available Sunday night between seven and twelve. The old man will have something for you to pick up around that time. Drive your truck when you go meet him. It's a good bit of material you got to pick up. Once you do that, I'm sure you know the routine from that point, right?" Mr. Raymond inquired.

"For sho, Ray. You know I got this," Mix replied.

"Yeah, I know you do. Now I got to call a few of my white guys to let them know to come on down in the next week or so to get their purchase. Be sure to keep your line open and stay available," Mr. Raymond lastly stated to Big Mix.

"I got you, Mr. Ray. It's a bet," Mix replied, and they ended the call.

The mission was for Mix to meet Emanuel that Sunday night to get all the product they had left along with the cash Emanuel was to fork over to Mr. Raymond. Then, Mix was to wait until the next morning and drive the product to a storage unit in Pompano Beach that they rented for that purpose, and await the customers Mr. Raymond had lined up to buy the product from the states he made mention of to Emanuel. Once the customers were to reach Florida, Mix and one or two of his cohorts would arrange to meet them at different hotels to deliver their goods and retrieve Mr. Raymond's cash. After that Mix would report back to Mr. Ray and give him his bread.

Mr. Raymond called Willie next. Willie was his other personal bodyguard. He was needed to come and pick him up to go and run a few errands and make a few stops. Mr. Raymond had some other business to square up prior to the planned vacation he had long wanted to take. It would last for two weeks and he had two destinations. His plan was to take Felicia along for the trip as he made rounds and conducted business. RayRay found himself completely in love with the short dark-skinned cutie with a big booty.

Felicia turned the old man out, and she utilized her sexual control to twist him in any direction she felt, like a thumb screw. Her head game and sexual skills were the bomb to Mr. Raymond, as he began to spend more time with her and away from home than he did with his wife. He absolutely enjoyed every moment he had with his mistress and promised to keep her in his corner until his dying day, so long as she intended to remain there. It benefited her well to do so. To keep loyal and true to Mr. Raymond.

Chapter 23

It was just past night fall as Parlay escorted his mother out of the supermarket and making their way to the Tahoe with groceries. All of a sudden, a masked gunman appeared from the blind-side of Parlay's vehicle and opened fire, hitting him in the right part of the chest.

Pow!

Parlay grabbed at the wound while his mother looked on in total shock. His legs began to give out as he withered to a collapse on his way the ground. The mother began shouting, but her voice wheezed out from panic. The gunman stood two feet away over him wielding a .357 magnum and determined to put an end to his life.

He fired another shot.

Pow!

Parlay was struck in the center of the chest this time.

Another shot was fired yet again.

Pow!

The assailant hit him in the chest once more, causing Parlay to pass out from the infliction of the lethal wounds.

The high-powered pistol was then planted flush against Parlay's forehead. He mumbled some words incoherently. The shooter pulled the trigger a fourth time to deliver a final shot. He blew off the front part of Parlay's head this go around.

Pow!

"Take that motherfucker! This is all for the team, you grimy cutthroat traitor son of a bitch!" the assassin mutter in broken English. He possibly was of Haitian-creole origin.

He then turned to Parlay's mother and pulled the trigger on her.

Pow!

He blew a hole in the head of Mrs. Irene, ending her life then and there. Afterwards, the gunman ran off, and was not seen by anyone as he fled . . . .

—

"*Ahhh! . . . Ahhh! . . . Ahhh!* What the fuck! What the hell! No! No!" shouted Parlay to the top of his lungs as he awaken in a cold sweat from the nightmare he was experiencing.

"Baby, baby, please! Calm down! Catch your breath, sweetie! You having a bad dream," Tisha said to him as they both now sat on the bed in the hotel suite. They were still out on their weekend date in Palm Beach. She wrapped her arms around him and began to rub his head and caress his body. "Everything is going to be alright, baby. I promise you. It's only a bad dream."

Parlay frantically looked around the hotel room as he slowly began to regain consciousness.

"Damn! A nigga don't need to have those type of dreams any fucking more, " he let out.

Tisha continued to caress his body as she kept hers pressed tightly against his. She kissed him gently on the cheeks, on the neck, and on the forehead, and then whispered into his ear. "Everything's going to be alright, sweetie. Just calm down," she said.

He turned his head and locked eyes with her as they kissed and then paused. "I'm good now, sweetie. I had one of the worst dreams I've ever had. I don't even want to speak on it because it was just that bad," he said.

"I wouldn't ever ask you to relate a bad dream to me no way, Melvin. I'm not that type of girl. Here, you want some more to eat," she said and stood to her feet allowing those voluptuous titties of hers to hang freely.

She walked over to the microwave to reheat the food he'd left over. As she sashayed across the floor, that thick ass of hers bobbled and jiggled so seductively that it caused him to instantly get a hard on once more. Before she'd put him to sleep, they'd gone at it for about an hour and thirty minutes non-stop. She sucked on the dick really good. He ate on the pussy even better. And they fucked like crazy as he managed to cum back to back. The Haitian American nympho Tisha, had some of the best pussy he'd ever had the pleasure to enjoy. Dude could honestly say that he was glad he'd taken a chance on being with Tisha. She definitely turned out to be worth it in many ways, especially sexually.

After he finished the remainder of the grub, they sat and indulged in an interesting conversation. "So, let me ask you. Tisha, what was it about me that really turned you on? I asked out of curiosity, so to gain a better understanding of your perception of me."

"Melvin, when you first came swaggering towards the bar, I took a liking to you right at that moment. You got this grand level of self-assurance about yourself, one like I haven't seen, and definitely never had the pleasure to experience with someone. You are a man's man, and I love that quality about you so much. You're a rare breed in this day and time, and on top of that, you keep yourself up in a major way. How could I lose by going after a dude like you? I had to take that chance. And now, here I am, giving you a slice of my cherry pie. How was it?" Tisha said with a sly giggle.

Parlay smiled at her words as he took a good look at her lovely face. She had one of the cutest pointed noses he'd seen on a female. Her face was smooth and radiant like a dark strip of silk with its round structure, puffy cheeks, and exquisite set of dimples. Tisha put you in the mind of the actress Gabriel Union, except with a pointed narrow nose and a darker complexion.

Their bodies complemented one another, and they had great chemistry. The thing he loved about her was that she knew exactly how to cater to him and on how to treat Parlay as the individual he was to her.

"So, what's the move with your dad? What's next on the agenda?" he inquired.

"Well, you know, my dad is pretty situated financially. The money's not a problem. That nigga has always been a supreme hustler, no doubt. He's got plans to buy the building that used to be the strip club called 'Black Gold' back in the day."

"You talking about the joint on Biscayne Boulevard, right?"

"Exactly. He's been in constant communication with the owner and has also thoroughly inspected the place to ensure all is well. He's been focused on that, among other things. He's really devastated and torn apart behind the bullshit that Ray pulled. I mentioned to him that you wanted to meet up and discuss a few things. He agreed. But then tried to dig into my personal life. He knows I got a thing for you. I guess it's some type of uncontrollable indicator about me that I give off. In a way, he seems to be okay with the thought of me having dealings with you, and on the other end, he has a problem fathoming it," Tisha related. "I don't truly know the answer to that. I guess it may be due to the fact that he knows how close Ray had brought you to him before he crossed my dad out, and he don't want me to have anything to do with someone that's tied to a snake. I can tell you one thing for damn sure, he don't know anything about us seeing each other, and I'm not about to allow him to dictate my love life for me either. It don't matter how close you and I get as a couple, I can't ever allow him to know the full extent of our relationship and dealings," Tisha stated.

"Our secret is safe with me," Parlay replied to her statement.

"Of course, I know it is. I still can't believe I gave myself to you so fast the way I did."

"Tisha, why you trying to front. You know you in love with this magic-stick I gave you," Parlay said as he grabbed hold of his manhood and wiggled it to a slight erection.

"Oh, yes, Melvin, you know I am," she said and then went down on him and took in a mouth full of his manhood. She ate up the gun for a good five minutes and then wanted to feel his nature deep inside of her once more.

"Melvin, come on. I want you to fuck me from the back, baby. I want you to fuck me good too, okay. Just like you did an hour or so ago," she stated in a matter-of-fact type of way.

He sat up on his knees atop the bed and had her to assume the position so he could pound deep in the pussy doggy style. Tisha got on all fours, arched her back deeply and raised her plumped ass in the air ready to be penetrated. He slapped her on the ass hard with his right hand and guided the way inside of her with the left. She quivered and attempted to run from him at first until he gripped her tightly by the hips with both hands and began to work gently as she enjoyed every stroke and bang of his pelvic smashing against her ass cheeks. They fucked until the both of them got dead-ass tired and fell completely asleep. Neither of the two didn't awake until later that Saturday evening.

They got dressed and went to a Jazz concert. From there they toured a museum and took part in the other festivities of the night life that Palm Beach had to offer before returning to the hotel. Tisha had everything perfectly planned and laid out for them to partake in. He could certainly get use to a woman that took pleasure in properly planning. Not saying that Traci didn't have those capabilities. She just didn't have that touch like Tisha had.

He began to dig deep into his own mind in the hopes of withdrawing a good lie that he was going to tell Traci about

RELENTLESS GOON | PRINCE A. TAUHID

his whereabouts and why had he been missing for the entire weekend, not simply for a day.

"You know something, Tisha?"

"What's that, baby?"

"You never did tell me much about Sekou or what happened between you two," he mentioned.

"Oh, my kids' father, huh?"

"Yeah, your kids' father," Parlay replied.

"Well, I couldn't take Sekou too much longer. He became too possessive, too controlling, and too abusive. I used to have to hide myself from my father and my family a lot after Sekou would beat me. Remember I told you he and my father were good friends and did business together in the underworld. My father would have killed him for sure had he known Sekou was beating on me the way he was. I couldn't have called him, nor could I have called the cops. I had to wait it out for fate to execute justice for me. Both of Sekou's parents were full-fledged Haitians that immigrated here. He was born on American soil and spoke both languages fluently. Sekou was a major member of the 'Zoe Pound' and had done a lot of things that was required of him according to the creed of the Zoes. My father's mother—my grandmother—is a high-powered Voodoo priestess who helped me out. I went to her and had roots put on Sekou to end his brutal assaults upon me and to punish him for all the times he had wronged me physically. Bottom-line is when the fall of the Zoe Pound came about and the feds came to round them up, Sekou got into a vicious shootout with them, and they gunned his ass down. That was six years ago. My oldest kid's nine, and my youngest is seven. We don't miss that motherfucker one bit. They never really knew him at the time he was killed, and I don't intend to make them aware of him either. I finally broke down and told my dad about all the ass-beatings Sekou used to put on me. That's why he's so overprotective about me and wants to be made known of anybody I fall in love with. So, like I said, we going to keep this on the low as best possible until the right time okay," Tisha stated.

"I'm with you on that, sweetie. But here is something else. I remember you mentioned more than once that your father and your kids' father were good business partners and whatnot in the underworld. You make me feel like it's a deeper message you trying to imply. What's the deal?" he asked in a straight forward way.

"Well, Melvin. Here is the deal on that. If I intend to fuck with you, I got to keep it real, right. Look, I love money, okay. Plain and simple. I love to make money. I love to help my man make money. And I love to spend money. I'm addicted to it. I love nice things, and I love to be treated like the queen that I am. My father has spoiled me and my sister our entire lives, and I will accept nothing less than what I'm used to, okay. Now, based on the fact that I chose you, and I want to be with you, I know I got to pull a few strings and make some moves to help build you up to full strength financially to take good care of me and my kids. And since you out of a job for the time being, I got to put you on, boo," Tisha stated.

Parlay played dumb to the fact of what she was really saying and then asked a seemingly crazy question. "What do you mean, put me on? How you intend to do that?"

"Before we even get into that, I want to know are you willing to put yourself out there again and get your grind on. I can supply you with everything you need, sweetie," she related.

"You can?"

"Damn right, boo. My father tied in with some major people down in Mexico."

"But I thought you don't want me to get close to your father in that type of way?"

"I don't. And you're not. Whenever you ready, I'm going to supply you with everything you need. And, if you didn't know, I have a few businesses I own and operate of my own.

I have a few hair salons, laundromats, a clothing store, and a few houses. Of course, you know my father and Sekou had financed everything, and I made sure to keep the businesses functioning well once I managed to make it to an independent position. I got some people that stay supplied through me. One of my cousins is tied in with my father, and he puts my money with his to get our product from my dad. My father knows nothing about my dealings. All he knows is that I'm doing good for myself through my establishments, and that I manage his money on a part-time basis. I've had anywhere from a half million to four million in cash at any one time. My family is into the new-wave of narcotics like meth, high grade weed, pills, and occasionally a few bricks of heroin."

"Damn, baby-girl! You been around the game for a minute, ain't you?"

"No, sweetie, I've been *in* the game for a minute!" Tisha retorted. "And I told you I love money, and definitely know how to get it. With my nigga or without him. I've been exposed to this lifestyle for so long, I had no choice but to get down. I'm in it to win it, playboy. Now, since we in the business of relating each other's business, what's up between you and Yolanda?" Tisha bluntly asked. She was looking only for straight answers.

"Oh that part. Nothing really. She was the one to introduce me to Mr. Raymond and your dad, and she was the one to help me get hired at the club."

"Melvin, don't lie to me. I see the way y'all admire each other and interact. I also see the way you smile at her and how she smiles back at you, so I figured it's got to be something deeper than what you telling me."

"Tisha, sweetie, real talk, I remember reading and studying from this philosophy book when I was in prison, and a quote that stood out to me directly related to the statement you just made."

"And what's that?"

"It said that, One of the single greatest evils to effect mankind, is that of speculation. It's never a good thing to speculate, baby. That's too much like being suspicious, and in most cases, suspicion is a sin."

"Well, okay, Mr. Student of Philosophy! I get your point. I just thought I'd ask. I don't want the joke to ever be on me, that's all."

"Tisha, look, sweetie. I'm not the type of nigga to play games with a woman. That shit ain't good. Besides, if Yolanda and I had anything going on, it would be me and her here, and not you and I. Need I say more on that," Parlay stated to get the last word in on her regarding such subject and move on to something else.

"Yeah, you got a point there, baby. I have to respect that. But anyway, I'm going to do all I can to support you and help make you a good business partner to my father without him knowing about us."

"You think you'll be able to balance that to perfection?" he asked.

"I'm sure I will," she replied.

"Good. Now about us getting to the money together. How soon?" he inquired.

"As soon as you tell me to go, baby. My people stay on deck."

"Word?"

"Word."

"Just hook it up between me and your father first. I don't want to get too side-tracked from the security thing that I wanted to get deeper into. I wouldn't mind making a career out of that, you know."

"Well, whatever. I'm with you. Now come on and let's make love some more while we got time. And you ain't got but two more condoms, so we going to make good use of them by the time it's all said and done," Tisha said as they got into the act of foreplay to stimulate one another and get back in the mood to a highly sexual charge.

They made it their business to fuck all throughout the night and showered together the next morning before checking out of the hotel. Dudebreally enjoyed those days he had with Tisha and the two of them all alone. They made the best of it and looked forward to more of the same at some point in the near future.

Chapter 24

Yolanda had not seen nor heard from her friend in months. Rachel had not called, texted, nor interacted on social media. Yolanda feared for her friend in the worst way as she took silent steps to help protect Rachel to no avail. She had prepared extensive witness statements in writing and audio recordings detailing everything Rachel had told her about the situation with her ex boyfriend. Once completed, she submitted the material anonymously to the office of the FBI in Texas that held jurisdiction over Houston, the city where Rachel's ex-boyfriend Santino lived, to bring them to the attention of the crimes she had been told that Santino committed and may be continuing to carry on. Yolanda also forwarded a copy of the key to them Rachel gave to her that went to the deposit box in LA. It had relevant evidence and other corroborated material locked inside.

Yolanda made Rachel a promise that she knew was bound to be broken. Being prevented by law, Yolanda was absolutely unable to deliver the money, the jewelry, or any other valuables that existed in the safe deposit box to the family or children of Rachel, for if she had, such actions would have made Yolanda a "party to a crime." Certain means would have to be taken to secure the finances Rachel's children needed to live off or prosper from, because under no circumstances were they to reap the benefits Rachel left, being in the event that something was to happen to her.

Yolanda played it safe on her end in multiple ways. The original key to the deposit box had been anonymously forwarded to the feds in LA as well to the appropriate authorities along with a statement notifying of the content and all other related Intel. Ever since the day Rachel reconnected with Yolanda, she had been busy trying to distance herself from Rachel in a sense, being that the FBI had her under their investigation along with Santino, and was possibly in the process of apprehending Rachel for the crimes she had committed. In the world of the Feds, "ignorance of the law is no excuse for anyone." Period. And Yolanda could not have afforded to jeopardize all that she had going on to assist Rachel.

Yolanda pulled out her cell phone and called Rachel's number, 786-972-0268:

"I'm sorry, you have reached a number that has been changed, disconnected, or no longer in service. If you feel you have reached this recording in error, please check the number and try your call again. Thank you."

Yolanda contacted Rachel's family next, and they hadn't seen or heard from her either. According to them, that was the "typical Rachel" as she had been through the years.

At the time that the state patrol impounded Rachel's car, a search of the vehicle was conducted. Her cell phone had been discovered and a few other items to help identify who possibly owned the car or who last drove it. Call data information was retrieved, and the last contact Rachel made was to the club she danced at, the night Wild Bill and C-Boy caught up to her. The phone was snatched from her hand and tossed back into the car falling between the seats. Not the slightest drop of evidence turned up to provide a trace to the whereabouts of Rachel. She was a goner and the hit team hired to do her in had done a fantastic job of kidnapping her, murking the bitch, and dumping her in a gator pit to be

RELENTLESS GOON | PRINCE A. TAUHID

devoured as a full course meal by the hungry reptiles. Santino was pleased with the work of his young gunners.

———

Traci found a way to gain Parlay's full attention again in a way unlike she had since his days of being free. She cooked meals now home-style. They were flavorfulnand nutritious to him. He was pleased with his woman because he'd simply grown sick and tired of those fast-food joints. Along with that, she revealed a deep and interesting desire to enter into culinary arts and have a catering business to reduce her hours of nursing work. Her vacation days were numerous, and we enjoyed almost a week together.

It was a fabulous Friday morning, and the two of them had tickets to a regular season basketball game for the Miami Heat. They were definitely eager to attend that night, as it was to be his first professional game appearance since his almost one year of being free. The night before, they'd fucked really good, ate a big bowl of ice cream together, and took advantage of her *Netflix* account like no other. It was memorable to say the least. Parlay had her ass climbing the walls and intensely calling out his name. After the fact, they had a much needed conversation.

At the oddest instance, it seemed that Tisha and Tina would text him as he spent quality time with Traci. He'd guessed it was one hell of a coincidence to have a thing for three ladies whose names start with the letter "T." But this turned out to be how life had it set up for him in this way.

At 12:30 that afternoon, he made a quick run to the fragrance shop near where Flea Market USA use to be on 79th Street to buy a few things. He wanted white tee shirts, socks, and to re-stock his fragrance collection of Muslim oils. Burberry sport was his favorite. Parlay wanted to continue to be the best representation of himself by and far.

—

The money from the sell of the club had cleared and was ready for transfers and other deposits. Several millions were transacted to Mexico, per orders of Mr. Raymond. Several other millions made its way to Zurich, Switzerland, and to a few other bank accounts in the Caribbean. Most notably, Turks and Caicos. One of Mr. Raymond's favorite vacation destinations. The FBI held pertinent interest in how the money was being moved, to further know the inner workings and dealings of their target Stephen's financial affairs. Two noteworthy names of female acquaintances appeared on the radar of the government that had exceptionally strong ties to their target. One was a Camille Hollande. And another, was a Felicia Nicole Brown. Both were mistresses of Mr. Raymond. He utilized the both of them to hide money in their names and start up business ventures under their signatures. A smart move on his behalf.

The aim of the government was to bring down the entire house of the Supreme Parliament, and everyone else involved once the gavel hits the surface. The ambition of the feds were to gather any and all information they could uncover. Therefore, they had to wait and allow things to further mount up on the crew so to leave NO WAY OUT at the point of the indictments being unsealed and arrests made. In other words, they wanted to give the Parliament enough rope for them to hang their own black asses by incriminating themselves. That was the concept and the strategy for the government to obediently adhere to, as the "Supreme Parliament" headed by Raymond Eugene Stephens, had no safety net in place to break the free-fall that they were bound to suffer.

Chapter 25

Mr. Raymond continued with enjoying the vacation he'd taken with his chief assistant Felicia, as the work at hand remained necessary to be carried out. There wasn't any problems on the end of the boss, being that he had multiple people who worked for him whom was only a phone call away. Also, he needed not do too much of the calling or conversing with others as instructions were dished out to his "play toy" assistant regarding who to call, what to say, where to be, when to be there, and how business was to be conducted. Felicia was exceptionally good at following his orders.

Mr. Raymond begun to teach, train, and groom Felicia on matters of being the personal secretary he desired her to be at any time they were alone. The duties that the wife was to be performing for him, had been placed in the hands of the mistress for many practical reasons. Mr. Raymond secretly held intentions to divorce Christine, but the marital problems that they faced couldn't have occurred at a more terrible time. The Mayoral race was two years away, and he needed not the affairs of his private life to go public, as this would've marred the campaign and potentially alienate the would-be voter base that he sought to build.

The other reason was that the beef and split he experienced with Mitch was about to get to cooking, and such spat would definitely cause harm to his bid. And lastly, the wife simply knew entirely too much regarding the criminal life of Mr. Raymond. And he held great fear that she would someday become his worst nightmare, by becoming the star witness for the Federal government.

Mr. Raymond further contemplated on his future as a politician, and the fears he faced regarding moving forward with his wife. He knew that a decision had to be reached long before election day, to either stay with Christine, or proceed forward with the divorce, being that he knew she wouldn't go for being separated. Such status may not register with the base of religious voters.

Mr. Raymond directed Felicia to call a particular female that she knew all too well, but had not seen since the doors to K.O.D. closed.

"Felicia, here, call this number for me from your line. It's Yolanda's. You remember her, right?" Mr. Raymond inquired, as he passed her his phone to read from the contact list.

"Of course, I remember her. She introduced me and helped me get going at the club," Felicia replied.

"Does she know about us?" Mr. Raymond had asked.

"I believe she's seen me in your office a time or two, and has a hunch that you and I may be more involved than simply boss and employee. Why you asked?" she questioned.

Agitated with the fact that she would question him, Mr. Raymond responded in a curmudgeon type fashion. "Never mind why I asked. Just answer the damn question," he retorted.

"Well, I'm sorry. My bad. You right. I shouldn't have asked that type of question," Felicia responded ghetto-like by moving her head and twisting her neck as she talked. "It won't happen again," she added and poked out her lips.

"Now, as I was saying, tell Yolanda that the money is available to be picked up, and to go to that spot I mentioned earlier. Be sure to text her first and say that it's me, Ray, and you are about to call. She should answer from that point."

Felicia did as she was told and contacted Yolanda.

Yolanda texted back and declared, "I'm available."

"Baby, she said yes, she's available to take the call," Felicia related to Mr. Raymond.

"Okay, good. Now call her and state my message verbally."

"What if she asks who am I?"

"Then you tell her it's you, and keep it simple as possible from there," Mr. Raymond stated. "Look, Lisa, what I'm trying to do is make it known in the best way possible that you are affiliated with me on a business level, until it's time to reveal our personal relationship, okay. I told you, I'm not letting you go nowhere, and I'm not going nowhere. We going to travel the world together and do good business on a major level. Just watch and see," Mr. Raymond said as he looked deep into Felicia's eyes, cupped her chin and pecked her on the lips passionately as he feed her solid words of encouragement and further placed the confidence in her mind that he had her back and would hold her down no matter what.

Felicia called Yolanda.

"Hello," she answered.

"Hey, is this Yolanda?" Felicia asked as she observed Mr. Ray from behind as he walked off towards the bar area on the beach to have his coconut refilled with the alcoholic drink he sipped on.

"Yes, this is Yolanda. Who is this?" Yolanda inquired.

"It's me, Yolanda, Lisa," Felicia replied.

"Lisa! Talking about short Lisa from the club? Nine-five-four and seven-zero-six Lisa," Yolanda inquired.

"Yes, that Lisa."

"I thought Mr. Ray text me from his number?"

"He did. I was told to do it for him. We're together."

"He's on vacation down in the Caribbean, ain't he?"

"*We* are on vacation together down in the Caribbean. I'm his new secretary. And for the purpose of taxes and all else, he brought me along to reap the benefit of having a tax write-off with the IRS," Felicia said to Yolanda, then had a thought to herself.

Ray said to be sure to keep it simple.

Yolanda quickly took heed of what was going on between Mr. Raymond and Felicia but didn't seek to get into it about things. She just kept to the business at hand.

"So, what's up, Lisa?" she stated.

"Mr. Ray told me to relate his words to you that the money is ready to be picked up. He said be sure to go by the location you're aware of today before nine tonight. His partner's waiting on you."

I know good and damn well, Mr. Ray has not put that girl in his business? Oh well. I guess that when he finally goes down, she'll go down right along with him, Special Agent Ursula Corbin thought to herself.

"Okay, let him know that I will. Also Lisa, I'm just curious to know, how long have you been the secretary for Mr. Ray?" Yolanda asked.

"It's been for quite some time now. No one never really knew. Those few times you saw me in his office, I was on the job as a secretary then."

"Oh, you were?"

"Yes, ma'am I was. I've been doing a very fine job ever since the first day that I began."

Felicia was implying on the low that she's been sexually pleasing Mr. Raymond ever since the day he desired to try her out.

"*Ohhh!* You don't say," Yolanda responded.

"Your introducing us really paid off," Felicia added.

"I see. But anyway, just let him know that I'll stop by today, and I thank him very dearly, okay."

"Will do. You take care girl," Yolanda concluded.

"Likewise," Felicia stated and pressed the end icon on the phone to kill the call.

Felicia sat in silence and held the phone in her hand as she overlooked the Caribbean sea while seated in her beach chair under the umbrella and deeply thought on ways to further empower herself through the acquaintance she had with Mr. Raymond as a mistress. She had much in common with him which she could benefit from, and personally sought ways to exploit her gold mine. *Now how shall I go about doing this?* Felicia thought.

—

At 7 p.m. that night, Yolanda made her way to the funeral chapel to meet up with Emanuel, the business associate of Mr. Raymond. Emanuel had one of his female associates on hand to communicate with Yolanda once she arrived. This acquaintance was there in the front lobby alone to await the visitor. Yolanda parked in the lot, got out of her BMW, and entered the establishment.

"Welcome to Fleming and Son Mortuary! How may I help you?" the niece of Emanuel, Angela, greeted.

"Yes, I'm here to see Mr. Emanuel, please," Yolanda replied.

"Hold on for a minute please," the niece stated and departed to a room in the back.

She returned moments later. "Right this way, ma'am," she stated, instructing Yolanda to follow her.

They went to the back and entered a small conference room that had a small table, two chairs and a stiff-faced Emanuel inside. The table had a nylon material bag on top that was zipped Closed. There was $200, 000 in cash within.

Emanuel's niece left him and Yolanda to themselves in the room to complete the business at hand.

"Hello! How are you?" Yolanda greeted.

"I'm well," Emanuel replied. "I understand you have something for me per Mr. Ray, my boss?"

"That's correct. I do. But for tax reasons, I have to ensure you sign these documents before you leave with this here money," Emanuel stated emphatically. He spoke in his old-fashioned tone as he handed Yolanda documents to sign.

She accepted and began to read over. Once the scanning of the paperwork was completed, she then signed, *Yolanda C. Harris.* Emanuel retrieved the papers, picked up the bag, and personally handed it to Yolanda.

"I wasn't told how much was supposed to be in there. He said you had knowledge of what you was to expect already," Emanuel stated.

"Thank you!" she stated, looking Emanuel in the eyes as she embraced the bag filled with money and attempted to turn and leave before Emanuel spoke again.

"I want to know something, if you will. How long have you and Ray known one another?" he inquired.

"Going on three years now," she replied.

"And what exactly *are* to him? And what do you do?" Emanuel further questioned.

"Well, my position at the time was to go out and recruit girls and talent to come work at the club. I helped to build the brand of the club and had the duty of management in my department. Mr. Ray and I are business acquaintances. Why might you ask?"

"Just thought I'd ask. Ray has had me give cash to people in the past, but never such large amount as this. Two hundred K in a lot of money, little lady. Twenty percent of a million dollars," Emanuel stated.

"And who are you to Mr. Ray?" Yolanda asked.

"Let's just say that I'm a longtime friend of the family, and not exclusively to Ray," Emanuel replied.

"Got you. I thank you, and you take care," Yolanda stated.

"And you do the same," Emanuel responded.

Yolanda departed and immediately reported to designated apartment up Interstate 95 away from Miami in Deerfield Beach, so to document, take photos, and report the entire transaction between her and Emanuel to her superiors. She had her iPhone on and audio recorded the conversation between the owner of the funeral parlor and herself as the device was hidden inside her purse. If only Mr. Raymond knew the type of harm and damage that he'd placed himself and Emanuel in by having Yolanda pick-up $200,000 in cash and exposing his silent business partner to someone he never truly knew at all. It was a terrible blunder by all means. One he could potentially suffer the consequences for later down the line.

—

Big Mix didn't have the slightest clue whatsoever that a tracking device had been placed under his vehicle. Mitch managed to outsmarted the opposition by having his nephew Roland, creep in throughout the middle of the night to the house of one of the personal security guards for Mr. Raymond, and plant the GPS gadget onto the vehicle of Mr. Raymond's occasional driver. The tool was very small, and if stashed properly, held a great potential to go undetected by the naked eye. Big Mix was never been mindful at no time to check for any such thing. Everything in the perimeters of the club, he had that part down to a science, but outside of that scope, he had a little more work to do.

Roland and three other henchmen followed the trail of the tracking device. They lag twenty minutes behind Big Mix. The plan was to kidnap dude, and torture him until he confessed all that he knew about Mr. Ray.

Big Mix made one stop in Pompano, prior to going to the hotel destination he was to lay over in Palm Beach. The room he had was on the lower level so as to have quicker access to his S.U.V. He checked into the room and pulled out his cell phone to make a few calls and send a text messages:

BIG MIX: Yo, Mr. Ray, I'm here. I'm in Pompano at the hotel. He text.

He let his boss know what his status was before he were to move on to the next stop and await the customers coming in from out of state.

He then texted Yolanda as he awaited the reply from Mr. Raymond.

BIG MIX: Hey Yolanda, it's me Mix. If you not too busy, give me a call.

Mix then picked up the remote to scan through the channels on the TV.

Yolanda was the first to reply.

YOLANDA: Hey Mix. What's up.

BIG MIX: Nothing too much. I had you on my mind. Can you talk? You available?

YOLANDA: Sure. Only for a few minutes though.

She responded like the many times before. Yolanda always allowed time for conversation with Big Mix, so he could run his mouth and further reveal things about Mr. Raymond to an unbeknownst federal agent, whom was determined to aide and assist in burying the drug Kingpin turned aspiring politician in prison for a long time to come.

Mix wasted no time to call, as he was eager to talk to Yolanda.

"Hey, Jerome! How are you, buddy," she answered.

"I've been well, Yolanda. How you been?" he returned the greeting?

"I'm just taking it one day at a time for now, since the majority of the excitement has not been attainable as it had during the good ol' days of K.O.D."

"Yeah, I know right. I don't know what made Mr. Ray put an end to all we had going on at the club, but things has really not been the same ever since. He did keep me on board to roll along with him for the next phase of his business ventures. But nothing would compare to King of Dimez, I don't believe," Mix stated. "He says he wants to make a run at becoming the Mayor. His interest is politics now. We've had personal conversations about it. Mr. Ray has his mind really made up, Yolanda. I only hope that he makes his peace with Mitch and kill the animosity that exists between the both of them. He and Mitch has rose from the mud together, and battled through the gutter to get to the point of putting their coins down in acquiring the land and the building that came to be known what it was. And I know for a fact that, their hands had to get dirty, and motherfuckers had to be eliminated in the process, before they were able to stand on a legitimate platform as owner and co-owner. Those two niggaz were once heavy in the game," Mix related.

"So, what caused Mr. Ray to severe ties?" Yolanda inquired.

"Truth be told, Yolanda, between me and you, it was some other shit going on behind the scenes of the club. As many times you have been in Mr. Ray's office and out with him one-on-one, I would think you may had known far more than I do," stated Mix.

"Not hardly, Mix. I was only in charge of bringing in the girls and the dance talent to the club, as we contributed to building and expanding the brand. While you on the other hand, was in charge of protecting the man's life, money, and property, big fella. Major difference there. And true indeed, you know Mr. Ray adored me and sought to have a personal understanding as we had. But Mix, mind you, I've always had to be the bigger person and draw the line on how far I would allow him to go with that, because I knew the dangers that comes along with mixing business and pleasure. This the same thing I be trying to tell you, Mix," Yolanda stated.

Yolanda knew the importance of getting the point across to her former co-worker but definitely had figured that Big Mix was not the type of guy to accept a no or snub for an answer. To stroke his ego and prevent him from being offended, she continued speaking to get him to talk more on the personal life and business hand Mr. Raymond had in the underworld.

"So, what's that part again about Mr. Ray and Mitch being heavy in the game and there being some behind the scenes issues that forced a separation?" Yolanda asked inquisitively. She now had the audio recorder on her cell phone activated.

"Like I said, it's some deep behind the scenes shit that took place, and Mr. Ray had to do something about it."

"Like what, Mix? Because I had never seen the two of them act as if they had on-going problems between each other. Everything appeared fine to me."

"Look, it went like this, Yolanda. You familiar with the movie *New Jack City*, right?"

"Of course, I am, Mix. I'm hood too."

"Okay, the beef between the two is similar to that of *Nino* and his brother *G-Money*. Mr. Ray is the man. Always has been and always will be. He inherited the throne from his eldest brother who died almost years ago."

"The brother whose vision it was to own a club and get out the game, right?" Yolanda chimed in.

"Right. How you know about that?" Mix asked.

"Mr. Ray has revealed many things to me, Mix. If a man wants a woman, he's got to make her familiar with who he is and what he do," Yolanda replied.

"You got a point there. But anyway, Mr. Ray put Mitch on and had supplied him for many years before the club thing. About three or four years ago, Mitch went and got connected to a different supplier. He began to cut side deals behind Mr. Ray's back. He would only use the money that he made at the club to go back in with Mr. Ray to re-up on supply as his input got reduced each time. Mr. Ray finally figured out what was going on when it was brought to his attention that Mitch's people who got rid of his product for him sold different material than Mr. Ray provided Mitch with. Anyway, to be one hundred percent sure that all he suspected was true, Mr. Ray went a month with no supply to sell while Mitch continued on selling the product he cut the side deal to get. He had even began building a team for himself outside of the dealers he and Mr. Ray already had in place. Mitch got a lot of Haitian and half Haitian niggaz behind him. And, if you noticed in the club, there was a divide between us on the security team. As you know, I'm Mr. Ray's guy and lead the pact, while Bo Jack was Mitch's guy. That nigga Mitch tried to move me out the way and put Bo Jack in my place. You know I had a problem with that."

"I know you did," Yolanda responded.

"But yeah, the two owners reached an agreement to have me and Bo Jack alternate days to hold leadership of security. Mr. Ray told me to not worry because some major changes would occur in due time."

"What type of problems did they have when I brought my guy Melvin to the club for the job," she sought to know.

"Mr. Ray was perfectly fine with it, because he was the one that told you to go out and find a guy, and the space needed to be filled. But Mitch had a problem with it at first, because he felt as though Mr. Ray was making too many moves and decisions over him, and they both had put up an equal share of the money to buy the club. He later started liking Melvin once he saw that he truly meant well and Melvin treated them both with the same amount of respect. I don't think Mitch is going to like it too much once he finds out how serious of a crush his daughter has on Melvin though," Mix related.

"Say what, Mix!" Yolanda replied in a way so to get the juicy details Mix now spoke on.

"Yeah, she crazy infatuated with dude. When he first started working, Tisha would ask me a thousand questions about him. I guess she finally got brave and found a way to make conversation with him. I wouldn't be surprised if he ain't already hit that by now, because I'm sure as head over heels that she was for the guy, she has definitely thrown herself at him some type of way, or is he yours to have like that?" Mix sarcastically stated.

"No, Mix. Me and Melvin have nothing going on personally," she retorted.

Good. That leaves the door open for me to try and get some of her sweet little juice box, he thought to himself.

"So, anyway, what you got in mind now that K.O.D. is no more?" Mix questioned.

"I made good from my work at King of Dimez. Mr. Ray cut the check and gave me my percentage. But I'm looking to continue on in the same line of work at Love Dolls. The owner Frank Nitty and Mr. Ray good friends. I'm sure you know that much?"

"I do," Mix responded.

"Mr. Ray put in a good word for me. And Nitty and I brokered a deal," Yolanda revealed to Mix.

"That's good to know. What you got going on in the next week or two? If you not too busy, can I take you out? I was thinking maybe we can enjoy a few margaritas for old times' sake like we once did as a family at the club."

"That sounds good, Mix. We *might* be able to do that. Let me see what my schedule looks like, and I'll let you know. But anyway, I've got to go now Mix. And it was nice talking to you, my friend."

"It was nice talking to you as well, Yolanda. Take care," Mix lastly stated.

"You do the same. Bye-bye," said Yolanda and the call ended.

Big Mix had done it yet again by revealing tidbits more of the criminal life Mr. Raymond and Mitch profited from than he was supposed to. Special Agent Corbin, knew without doubt that Jerome Arthur Maxwell, aka "Big Mix" knew far more about the criminal activities of his boss and the cohort than he was willing to reveal over the phone. In order for her to get him to spill his guts as never before, she would have to forge a situation where they would share a private session together, and she would perpetuate a silent "non-existent" competition for her pleasure between him and Mr. Ray. She would need to even dash a few lies into the equation and sprinkle a little slander on the ears of them both, to pit boss and bodyguard at odds against each other. The likelihood of her strategy to be successful was high. She would need to employ such methods in due time. If she sought to gain a great lead to speed up the process of having them indicted.

Big Mix visited a few social media websites through the apps on his phone once the conversation with Yolanda ended. Roland and his team finally made it to the hotel location and spotted Mix's S.U.V. He drove a dark blue Yukon Denali with heavy tint. Now all that was necessary was to find out what room Mix was situated, so they could go in on him, take him hostage, and make him speak on the stash spots of the money and drugs.

Roland had to think of something quick so to not draw suspicion to him and the three other black males in a Chevy Suburban stationed in the parking lot of a hotel for no apparent reason. He felt as though Mix couldn't be too many doors away from his truck, being that Mix was the type of guy that always liked to have speedy access to his vehicle, according to Mitch. How would he go about accomplishing what he had set out to do?

Roland finally thought up an idea. Being that Mix didn't know too much about him and hadn't seen his face, he would drop his cohorts off at some low budget motel to be out of sight, then return to the location shortly after where Mix was situated. He would then await the parking space to open on either side of Mix's truck and attempt to back in, but purposely have a fender-bender and dent the rear end of Mix's Yukon, causing the alarm to go off and compelling Mix to come out and assess the damage to his vehicle. They would immediately come to an agreement with one another, being that neither of the two wanted the cops to get involved. Roland knew Mix potentially had drugs in the truck. Roland would then need to leave the room Mix rested in, and he and his boys would later return and go in on him and take dude hostage.

That was plan A. Plan B would require Roland and his guys to simply pull up on Mix four deep in their vehicle as added muscle, and force Big Mix out of his ride and swiftly into the one they traveled in. It would be necessary for them to wait for him to leave the room and get in his ride. Then they would have to allow him opportunity to go down the road a block or two, pass his vehicle in theirs, and get in front of him as he drove down the street. Instantly, Roland would jam on the brakes and cause Mix to run into the rear of his vehicle. This was the secondary plan Roland held in mind, only if the first fell apart. But no matter what, the overall objective was to subdue Mix, and pull over to the side of the road out of traffic, draw down on Mix with their guns, and force him into the back of their vehicle, as another jumped into the driver seat of Mix's ride. They'd drive off with both the kidnapped victim and his vehicle. Roland chose to go with plan A, but would include an added twist to it. The plan was to be put into effect that night.

Roland and crew left the parking lot of the hotel en route to a low budget resting spot in the area. The time was 10:17 p.m. He and his boys planned to return after midnight.

—

The time reached 12:41 a.m., and Roland returned along with his crew. Mix's truck was still parked in the same location. Roland had one of his men to go over and poke a hole in the back left rear tire of Mix's truck. He also had two of the others to get out and head across the street until they was to see Mix exit the hotel room and begin to change the rear tire after looking at the damage that Roland would cause following backing into his vehicle. The plan was in place and they took action.

Wham!

Roland backed into the rear end of Mix's truck, causing a medium-sized dent in the process, and forcing the alarm to begin blaring. Roland left his truck parked two feet from the back of Mix's truck bumper facing in the opposite direction with the rear door unlocked and at the ready to have Mix tossed inside.

The alarm system on Mix's truck had a distinct sound to it to make him absolutely know that it was his vehicle's alerts that was going off. He appeared from the room three doors down from the parking space he occupied.

Boc-Boc!

The alarm to his vehicle was silenced by the push of a button on the key chain remote. Mix approached to take note of what was going on.

"What the fuck! You backed into my truck, dude!" Big Mix said.

"My bad bro. I was trying to back in but couldn't see that well, and I ended up making a mistake and bumped into your whip," Roland responded.

"And you put a nice sized dent in my shit too, huh! I hope you got some good insurance, because you got to pay for this bullshit right here, homeboy. And how the fuck my tire get flat?" Mix stated once he observed the deflated wheel.

"I don't know about that one there. I'll take the blame for the dent though. But I had nothing to do with the tire being flat," Roland responded to Mix about his back tire.

It came to Big Mix's mind that he was loaded with narcotics and absolutely could not afford for the police to report to the scene at any time or under any circumstances. He figured that the best thing to do was to resolve the situation as fast as possible, get the responsible person away from him, retrieve his tire jack and spare from the rear of his truck, change it out, and proceed forward with his business at hand. He squatted to take a look at the tire. He rubbed his hand along it to see if or not a nail or some other sharp object was still stuck within.

"Damn! I had to run over something to cause this flat," Mix stated.

"You must have. But about the dent that I caused. How can we deal with this without having the police come out taking reports and trying to make shit out to be bigger than what it is? Also, I don't need my insurance company raising my rate due to some minute accident," Roland said to Mix.

"I don't know. We'll figure something out. I got to change this damn tire too. My ass ain't even got a jack. Fuck! Now I got to call my brother or somebody to drive here to help me with that," Mix stated.

"No need to stress on that. I got a jack. I can help you with it" Roland replied.

"I ain't got a spare either," Mix lied so he wouldn't have to enter the back of his truck and possibly expose the content of material in his possession to the stranger.

"No need to worry about that either. Both of our trucks are made by GMC, so I'm sure the spare I have will fit the wheelbase. We could just knock off some of the pay I owe you for the dent by me giving you the spare," Roland proposed.

"That's a bet," Mix agreed, completely oblivious to what was truly going on and unable to detect the trap that was being set to catch him.

Roland went to the rear of his truck and got the jack and the spare. He passed the tools to Mix, as he began to work on replacing his tire. As Mix swapped out wheels, Roland text his other two guys a quick message to alert them that they were about to take the big fella down, and for them to begin walking in the direction.

Roland had an additional lug-wrench in the spare tire section of his truck that he imagined would be utilized if necessary. He took a look down at Mix and saw that he only had two lugs left before finishing the job of changing out tires. He then looked up and observed his other two cohorts not far away from reaching them. Mix had his back to them and his head low, focused on the work he sought to complete as quickly as possible.

Wham! . . . Wham-Wham-Wham-Wham!

Roland waylaid Big Mix, clocking him on the back of his head four times viciously with the second lug tool he slyly retrieved. Mix was out cold and snoring. Roland's partner that sat in the passenger seat immediately hopped out and began helping to lift Mix from the pavement as they began attempting to toss him in the back of Roland's Suburban. He was too heavy. Roughly fifteen seconds later, the other two appeared, and then all four of them were able to easily scoop the giant and throw him on board. Mix was chest and face to the floor.

"JT, tape this nigga up quickly!" Roland ordered.

Roland himself then ran Mix's pockets so to get his truck keys. "Here, Nick." He tossed the keys. "Finish putting that other lug bolt on and drive this nigga's truck to the spot. We out of here. Be sure to take a good look around to be aware no one seen shit," Roland dictated and then hit the gas on the powerful S.U.V. he drove.

Nick did as ordered and lagged behind the crew maybe eight to ten minutes. Their destination was a house in Davie, Florida where Mitch occasionally used as a safe house. It had a garage to it with a door to conceal probing eyes from peeping inside. The house was also somewhat off to itself and not too close to any neighbors.

JT was sure to tape Mix's feet together and his hands behind his back once he tied him well with a double pair of shoelaces.

Once inside, the kidnapping crew communicated with each other.

"You took care of that back there, JT?" Roland asked.

"I'm done," JT replied.

"Good. Now take that nigga's shoes off, get his socks, stuff them in his mouth and tape them tight to keep his ass from screaming or talking," Roland further dictated.

"I'm on it." JT did as told and then ran Mix's pockets yet a second time, taking everything he had. JT got his phone and his wallet. Mix had about $2,800 in cash. They really had Mix down bad and fucked up. He knew not the slightest thing that was going on with him. Roland had a bag of towels in the Suburban that he used to dry the vehicle off whenever he detailed it. JT took four of them and placed them around Mix's head to stop the bleeding. Everyone sat in silence in the house as they awaited Mitch's arrival. Once he was to get there, the additional dirty work was to begin. The torture of their kidnapped victim. They would be in for a big surprise that was sure to please them, and Mitch. They would soon discover the material that was in Mix's truck, along with the information that they were to gather from his phone. Advantage: TEAM MITCH.

Epilogue

Parlay began to have hunger pangs like he'd never had before. He craved the flavor and taste of some famous *Popeye's* fried chicken. It was 10:07 p.m., on a Wednesday night, and he had to get to the nearest Popeye's before closing time.

Once there he ordered a breast, two wings, two biscuits, and bowl of dirty rice. He also ordered a large sweet tea. Since he didn't have anywhere to be, and wanted to devour the food he'd been craving peacefully, dude decided to chill and eat his food there.

Although Parlay was subject to a strip search or obligated to provide a urine sample at any time due to the Federal probation, he didn't really give a fuck to much about it. He felt the need to keep protection on his person. Who knew? The past was always uglier than the present for some people. And karma didn't give a damn how she was to get to you, so long as she did. So, with that thought in mind, Parlay bought two pistols from his cousin Vick. One was a Ruger P89 and the other was a Colt .45 with a pearl handle, just like the one he'd seen Mr. Raymond with when he first met him. A lot of people might say that he was operating stupidly for having guns while being fresh from prison and a convicted felon on supervision. However, he felt as though he had entirely too much to fear, and may have had far more enemies from his past than he realized. He had to have some protection and remain strapped. At all cost.

195

Parlay had the Ruger tucked along his waistband as always before leaving the house. The mean and unapologetic streets of Miami, Florida would forever and a day keep a steady flow of money-hungry street niggaz on the prowl, looking to rob people, or execute a double-dose of revenge on a enemy. Before his arrest, he'd made mental note of all the nigga, whom he felt may pose a threat on his life. He had been involved in too many shootouts and had actually hit a few people during those times.

As Parlay was eating and checking out the females who worked there, he absolutely couldn't believe his motherfucking eyes at who it was he saw in the moment. It was that pussy-ass nigga Calvin Prescott that walked through the front door of the place. The nigga who snitched on him to the feds and had his ass sent to prison. That rat-ass nigga sang gospel songs to the to the government. Dude had picked up weight and was a little puffy in the cheeks. Nonetheless, Parlay was still able to identify who he was without a doubt. Dude was dressed in run down clothes and had a head full of nappy-ass hair. Even if Calvin had turned and looked in the direction where Parlay sat, he probably wouldn't have known it was him, due to Parlay having grown a full beard, and the thirty pounds of added muscle he'd put on. He had on a hat too, pulled low over his eyes.

The short female cashier that took Calvin's order confirmed his identity.

"Hey, Calvin! What's good? What you eating on tonight?" she asked.

"Hey there! How you doing? Let me get a mixed twelve piece with biscuits, two large orders of dirty rice, and four extra large lemonades to go," he stated.

"I got you," the female with the name tag Shonda replied.

"I got to use the bathroom right quick."

"Okay, go ahead. I'll have your order ready by the time you get back."

"Bet that," Calvin replied, then made his way to relieve himself.

Parlay had not seen that bitch-ass nigga since the day he last walked out of the courtroom with his lenient sentence and a smile. He was one person whom he would never be able to forget. Not even if he prayed to do so.

Being that he now had Calvin's bitch-ass directly in his sights and held one of his pistols on him, the only question that remained was . . . *What was he now going to do to avenge the treachery Calvin perpetrated against him?*

An extreme rush of rage shot through Parlay's body, as his psyche was pushed beyond the brink of insanity. Dude had become a bit unhinged between reality and make-believe. He had total access to Calvin at the moment and could do whatever he so pleased to exact justice upon the boy. Why did Parlay have to be placed in such a predicament? He assumed that fate had a funny way of drawing back and releasing its arrows in the direction of those that were subject to get it.

He continued to keep his head low, making the decision to take advantage of the opportunity afforded to me. Parlay got to his feet and exited the restaurant to lie in wait for Calvin to walk out.

Yeah, I'm about to get his ass! I can't let that shit go! Not any longer! I'm about to shoot the shit out of this pussy-ass nigga! he thought to himself.

His mind had so much going on in it as he sat behind the wheel of the rental. He cared about nothing any longer. He was determined that he simply had to get him.

Parlay observed Calvin through the front window of the restaurant. He'd come out the restroom and gotten his order. As he got back into his car and took off out the parking lot, Parlay was hot on his tail, like a blue tick hound in chase of a coon on the first day of hunting season.

Parlay followed closely behind Calvin. He noticed him pull out his cell phone. He'd began to talk with someone.

As Parlay continued to follow, with his eyes locked in on him and gritting his teeth, he eased out his pistol. His breathing intensified, and he'd lost all sense of control. Absolutely nothing mattered in that moment other than shooting that fuck-nigga, Calvin!

Parlay experienced an adrenaline many times in his past through similar situations, so when the moment became the moment, there wasn't no pressure. The track *"100 I Shute 2"* from the album *"GHETTout"* by rapper *Starlito* pumped from the speakers in the rental Parlay drove. That was one of his favorite songs there.

He was about four to five car lengths behind Calvin. Judging by the route dude took, it appeared Calvin was headed to his momma's house. She lived in the same spot for twenty plus years now. Once he turned onto her street, Parlay knewnwithout doubt, he was to soon come to a stop.

Calvin pulled up to the curb. Once the headlights went off, he the engine had been cut off. Parlay slowed to creep down the street. Once close enough, he let the passenger window down fully. Moments prior to, Parlay had wrapped the plastic bag from Popeyes around his hand as he clutched the pistol. Once he was to began blasting, he'd be able to trap the shell casings from the bullets. He still maintained that he simply had to get that nigga! He couldn't let it go. For nothing in the world. Calvin was the one responsible for all the fuck shit to have happened to him and his daughter, Parlay felt. And he was the reason dude couldn't be there to protect and defend Sherita. The fucked up shit that the nigga Charles did to her, probably wouldn't have ever occurred, had he been free. The man's thoughts ran wild. And he couldn't let him off the hook. Not for once.

Parlay pulled the rental alongside the car Calvin drove, noticing that the intended target was on the phone. It was pinned to his ear as he leaned over into the passenger seat to get the bags of food he had. Calvin talked loud enough on the phone to some other dude that Parlay was able to hear all they discussed. The phone was on speaker.

"Aye Lo, boy you crazy, my nigga! How you say you had that bitch up in the motel room again, now?" Calvin asked of his partner Carlos.

"Man . . . I had that hoe sucking on good dick, boy! She was the best at what she do!"

"Oh yeah! What she—"

Boom-Boom-Boom-Boom-Boom! . . . *Boom!* . . . *Boom-Boom-Boom!* . . . *Boom-Boom!*

Calvin's words were cut short by a hail of gunfire.

Parlay let off *seven to eight shots. Maybe nine? he thought to himself.*

The bottom line was that, he gave it to that bitch-ass nigga, Calvin Prescott! Just as he'd long wanted to do.

Parlay felt for sure that he'd hit the nigga in the *head*, the *chest*, and elsewhere about the body. But did he really? He would never know until the official report was to be made on the news later after the fact.

So much for the life of Calvin, the rat he'd came to be. Karma returned to snatch her measure of justice against him. And besides, the code of the streets was that, all rats must die! Even the most legendary and most infamous snitches would eventually get it, no matter how long it's been since they told, or where so ever they shall be. Period!

TO BE CONTINUED

COMING SOON IN THE SERIES

RELENTLESS II
Gritty, Gutter, Grimy, Murderous

RELENTLESS III

Synopsis to Relentless . . .

From prison, Melvin Anderson, aka "Parlay," returns to society in Miami Florida, determined to rise again. Within his first hours of freedom, he's approached by a female, a Yolanda Harris. There's something alluring about her, yet mysterious. She has involvement at the hottest strip-club in all the south. Ownership needed additional security. Yola held duty to "find them a guy." Interest was placed in Parlay, among other things.

The club's primary owner, Mr. Raymond Stephens, has a friendship and business relation in Mitchell Duvalier-Collins, aka "Long Money Mitch." They both used Illicit funds to buy the club. The duo is heavy in the game by and far.

Mr. Ray inherited his empire. Eventually he grows tired of it all. He desires to become a politician, and holds ambition to be Mayor Of Miami. Mitch has no desire to do as Ray. He wants to expand the club's brand and continue to move forward in the drug trade.

A bitter split takes place, leaving Yolanda and Parlay choosing sides. Through it all, Yolanda has other duties to carry out.

Parlay reunites with his cousin Vick, whose now heavily moving firearms and ammunition through the "Iron Pipeline." Vick seeks to convince Parlay to roll along. Parlay has a choice to make. One he simply couldn't refuse. He loved the fast life and easy money.

The federal government has a hard-on for Mr. Raymond and his organization. Certain methods hadn't worked. Others are to be utilized in the hopes to take him down. Parlay is totally unaware of it all.

Love Is Lost . . . Betrayal Is Heavy . . . Blood Is Shed . . . And disloyalty Is Rampant! Battle for supremacy is fought on four different fronts here. Who shall prevail?

Lock Down Publications and Ca$h Presents
Assisted Publishing Packages

BASIC PACKAGE	UPGRADED PACKAGE
$499	$800
Editing	Typing
Cover Design	Editing
Formatting	Cover Design
	Formatting
ADVANCE PACKAGE	**LDP SUPREME PACKAGE**
$1,200	$1,500
Typing	Typing
Editing	Editing
Cover Design	Cover Design
Formatting	Formatting
Copyright registration	Copyright registration
Proofreading	Proofreading
Upload book to Amazon	Set up Amazon account
	Upload book to Amazon
	Advertise on LDP, Amazon and Facebook Page

***Other services available upon request.
Additional charges may apply

Lock Down Publications
P.O. Box 944
Stockbridge, GA 30281-9998
Phone: 470 303-9761

Submission Guideline

Submit the first three chapters of your completed manuscript to ldpsubmissions@gmail.com. In the subject line add **Your Book's Title**. The manuscript must be in a Word Doc file and sent as an attachment. Document should be in Times New Roman, double spaced, and in size 12 font. Also, provide your synopsis and full contact information. If sending multiple submissions, they must each be in a separate email.

Have a story but no way to send it electronically? You can still submit to LDP/Ca$h Presents. Send in the first three chapters, written or typed, of your completed manuscript to:

LDP: Submissions Dept
P.O. Box 944
Stockbridge, GA 30281-9998

DO NOT send original manuscript. Must be a duplicate. Provide your synopsis and a cover letter containing your full contact information.

Thanks for considering LDP and Ca$h Presents.

NEW RELEASES

BLOODLINE OF A SAVAGE **BY PRINCE A. TAUHID**

THE MURDER QUEENS 4 **BY MICHAEL GALLON**

THE BUTTERFLY MAFIA **BY FUMIYA PAYNE**

KING KILLA 2 **BY VINCENT "VITTO" HOLLOWAY**

BABY, I'M WINTERTIME COLD 3 **BY MEESHA**

THESE VICIOUS STREETS **BY PRINCE A. TAUHID**

TIL DEATH 2 **BY ARYANNA**

CITY OF SMOKE 2 **BY MOLOTTI**

STEPPERS **BY KING RIO**

THE LANE **BY KEN-KEN SPENCE**

MONEY GAME 2 **BY SMOOVE DOLLA**

THE BLACK DIAMOND CARTEL **BY SAYNOMORE**

CRIME BOSS 2 **BY PLAYA RAY**

THUG OF SPADES **BY COREY ROBINSON**

LOVE IN THE TRENCHES 2 **BY COREY ROBINSON**

TIL DEATH 3 **BY ARYANNA**

THE BIRTH OF A GANGSTER 4 **BY DELMONT PLAYER**

PRODUCT OF THE STREETS **BY DEMOND "MONEY" ANDERSON**

Coming Soon from Lock Down Publications/Ca$h Presents

BLOOD OF A BOSS VI
SHADOWS OF THE GAME II
TRAP BASTARD II
By **Askari**

LOYAL TO THE GAME IV
By **T.J. & Jelissa**

TRUE SAVAGE VIII
MIDNIGHT CARTEL IV
DOPE BOY MAGIC IV
CITY OF KINGZ III
NIGHTMARE ON SILENT AVE II
THE PLUG OF LIL MEXICO II
CLASSIC CITY II
By **Chris Green**

BLAST FOR ME III
A SAVAGE DOPEBOY III
CUTTHROAT MAFIA III
DUFFLE BAG CARTEL VII
HEARTLESS GOON VI
By **Ghost**

A HUSTLER'S DECEIT III
KILL ZONE II
BAE BELONGS TO ME III
TIL DEATH II
By **Aryanna**

KING OF THE TRAP III
By **T.J. Edwards**

GORILLAZ IN THE BAY V
3X KRAZY III
STRAIGHT BEAST MODE III
By **De'Kari**

KINGPIN KILLAZ IV
STREET KINGS III
PAID IN BLOOD III
CARTEL KILLAZ IV
DOPE GODS III
By **Hood Rich**

SINS OF A HUSTLA II
By **ASAD**

YAYO V
BRED IN THE GAME 2
By **S. Allen**

THE STREETS WILL TALK II
By **Yolanda Moore**

SON OF A DOPE FIEND III
HEAVEN GOT A GHETTO III
SKI MASK MONEY III
By **Renta**

LOYALTY AIN'T PROMISED III
By **Keith Williams**

I'M NOTHING WITHOUT HIS LOVE II
SINS OF A THUG II
TO THE THUG I LOVED BEFORE II
IN A HUSTLER I TRUST II
By **Monet Dragun**

QUIET MONEY IV
EXTENDED CLIP III
THUG LIFE IV
By **Trai'Quan**

THE STREETS MADE ME IV
By **Larry D. Wright**

IF YOU CROSS ME ONCE III
ANGEL V
By **Anthony Fields**

THE STREETS WILL NEVER CLOSE IV
By **K'ajji**

HARD AND RUTHLESS III
KILLA KOUNTY IV
By **Khufu**

MONEY GAME III
By **Smoove Dolla**

MURDA WAS THE CASE III
Elijah R. Freeman

AN UNFORESEEN LOVE IV
BABY, I'M WINTERTIME COLD III
By **Meesha**

QUEEN OF THE ZOO III
By **Black Migo**

CONFESSIONS OF A JACKBOY III
By **Nicholas Lock**

JACK BOYS VS DOPE BOYS IV
A GANGSTA'S QUR'AN V
COKE GIRLZ II
COKE BOYS II
LIFE OF A SAVAGE V
CHI'RAQ GANGSTAS V
SOSA GANG III
BRONX SAVAGES II
BODYMORE KINGPINS II
By **Romell Tukes**

KING KILLA II
By **Vincent "Vitto" Holloway**

BETRAYAL OF A THUG III
By **Fre$h**

THE MURDER QUEENS III
By **Michael Gallon**

THE BIRTH OF A GANGSTER III
By **Delmont Player**

TREAL LOVE II
By **Le'Monica Jackson**

FOR THE LOVE OF BLOOD III
By **Jamel Mitchell**

RELENTLESS GOON | PRINCE A. TAUHID

RAN OFF ON DA PLUG II
By **Paper Boi Rari**

HOOD CONSIGLIERE III
By **Keese**

PRETTY GIRLS DO NASTY THINGS II
By **Nicole Goosby**

PROTÉGÉ OF A LEGEND III
LOVE IN THE TRENCHES II
By **Corey Robinson**

IT'S JUST ME AND YOU II
By **Ah'Million**

FOREVER GANGSTA III
By **Adrian Dulan**

GORILLAZ IN THE TRENCHES II
By **SayNoMore**

THE COCAINE PRINCESS VIII
By **King Rio**

CRIME BOSS II
By **Playa Ray**

LOYALTY IS EVERYTHING III
By **Molotti**

HERE TODAY GONE TOMORROW II
By **Fly Rock**

REAL G'S MOVE IN SILENCE II
By **Von Diesel**

GRIMEY WAYS IV
By **Ray Vinci**

Available Now

RESTRAINING ORDER I & II
By **CA$H & Coffee**

LOVE KNOWS NO BOUNDARIES I II & III
By **Coffee**

RAISED AS A GOON I, II, III & IV
BRED BY THE SLUMS I, II, III
BLAST FOR ME I & II
ROTTEN TO THE CORE I II III
A BRONX TALE I, II, III
DUFFLE BAG CARTEL I II III IV V VI
HEARTLESS GOON I II III IV V
A SAVAGE DOPEBOY I II
DRUG LORDS I II III
CUTTHROAT MAFIA I II
KING OF THE TRENCHES
By **Ghost**

LAY IT DOWN I & II
LAST OF A DYING BREED I II
BLOOD STAINS OF A SHOTTA I & II III
By **Jamaica**

LOYAL TO THE GAME I II III
LIFE OF SIN I, II III
By **TJ & Jelissa**

IF LOVING HIM IS WRONG…I & II
LOVE ME EVEN WHEN IT HURTS I II III
By **Jelissa**

BLOODY COMMAS I & II
SKI MASK CARTEL I, II & III
KING OF NEW YORK I II, III IV V
RISE TO POWER I II III
COKE KINGS I II III IV V
BORN HEARTLESS I II III IV
KING OF THE TRAP I II
By **T.J. Edwards**

WHEN THE STREETS CLAP BACK I & II III
THE HEART OF A SAVAGE I II III IV
MONEY MAFIA I II
LOYAL TO THE SOIL I II III
By **Jibril Williams**

A DISTINGUISHED THUG STOLE MY HEART I II &
III
LOVE SHOULDN'T HURT I II III IV
RENEGADE BOYS I II III IV
PAID IN KARMA I II III
SAVAGE STORMS I II III
AN UNFORESEEN LOVE I II III
BABY, I'M WINTERTIME COLD I II
By **Meesha**

A GANGSTER'S CODE I &, II III
A GANGSTER'S SYN I II III
THE SAVAGE LIFE I II III
CHAINED TO THE STREETS I II III
BLOOD ON THE MONEY I II III
A GANGSTA'S PAIN I II III
By **J-Blunt**

PUSH IT TO THE LIMIT
By **Bre' Hayes**

RELENTLESS GOON | PRINCE A. TAUHID

BLOOD OF A BOSS I, II, III, IV, V
SHADOWS OF THE GAME
TRAP BASTARD
By **Askari**

THE STREETS BLEED MURDER I, II & III
THE HEART OF A GANGSTA I II& III
By **Jerry Jackson**

CUM FOR ME I II III IV V VI VII VIII
An **LDP Erotica Collaboration**

BRIDE OF A HUSTLA I II & II
THE FETTI GIRLS I, II& III
CORRUPTED BY A GANGSTA I, II III, IV
BLINDED BY HIS LOVE
THE PRICE YOU PAY FOR LOVE I, II ,III
DOPE GIRL MAGIC I II III
By **Destiny Skai**

WHEN A GOOD GIRL GOES BAD
By **Adrienne**

A GANGSTER'S REVENGE I II III & IV
THE BOSS MAN'S DAUGHTERS I II III IV V
A SAVAGE LOVE I & II
BAE BELONGS TO ME I II
A HUSTLER'S DECEIT I, II, III
WHAT BAD BITCHES DO I, II, III
SOUL OF A MONSTER I II III
KILL ZONE
A DOPE BOY'S QUEEN I II III
TIL DEATH
By **Aryanna**

214

THE COST OF LOYALTY I II III
By Kweli

A KINGPIN'S AMBITION
A KINGPIN'S AMBITION **II**
I MURDER FOR THE DOUGH
By **Ambitious**

TRUE SAVAGE I II III IV V VI VII
DOPE BOY MAGIC I, II, III
MIDNIGHT CARTEL I II III
CITY OF KINGZ I II
NIGHTMARE ON SILENT AVE
THE PLUG OF LIL MEXICO II
CLASSIC CITY
By **Chris Green**

A DOPEBOY'S PRAYER
By **Eddie "Wolf" Lee**

THE KING CARTEL I, II & III
By **Frank Gresham**

THESE NIGGAS AIN'T LOYAL I, II & III
By **Nikki Tee**

GANGSTA SHYT I II &III
By **CATO**

THE ULTIMATE BETRAYAL
By **Phoenix**

BOSS'N UP I, II & III
By **Royal Nicole**

RELENTLESS GOON | PRINCE A. TAUHID

I LOVE YOU TO DEATH
By **Destiny J**

I RIDE FOR MY HITTA
I STILL RIDE FOR MY HITTA
By **Misty Holt**

LOVE & CHASIN' PAPER
By **Qay Crockett**

TO DIE IN VAIN
SINS OF A HUSTLA
By **ASAD**

BROOKLYN HUSTLAZ
By **Boogsy Morina**

BROOKLYN ON LOCK I & II
By **Sonovia**

GANGSTA CITY
By **Teddy Duke**

A DRUG KING AND HIS DIAMOND I & II III
A DOPEMAN'S RICHES
HER MAN, MINE'S TOO I, II
CASH MONEY HO'S
THE WIFEY I USED TO BE I II
PRETTY GIRLS DO NASTY THINGS
By Nicole Goosby

LIPSTICK KILLAH I, II, III
CRIME OF PASSION I II & III
FRIEND OR FOE I II III
By **Mimi**

TRAPHOUSE KING I II & III
KINGPIN KILLAZ I II III
STREET KINGS I II
PAID IN BLOOD I II
CARTEL KILLAZ I II III
DOPE GODS I II
By **Hood Rich**

STEADY MOBBN' I, II, III
THE STREETS STAINED MY SOUL I II III
By **Marcellus Allen**

WHO SHOT YA I, II, III
SON OF A DOPE FIEND I II
HEAVEN GOT A GHETTO I II
SKI MASK MONEY I II
By **Renta**

GORILLAZ IN THE BAY I II III IV
TEARS OF A GANGSTA I II
3X KRAZY I II
STRAIGHT BEAST MODE I II
By **DE'KARI**

TRIGGADALE I II III
MURDA WAS THE CASE I II
By **Elijah R. Freeman**

THE STREETS ARE CALLING
By **Duquie Wilson**

SLAUGHTER GANG I II III
RUTHLESS HEART I II III
By **Willie Slaughter**

RELENTLESS GOON | PRINCE A. TAUHID

GOD BLESS THE TRAPPERS I, II, III
THESE SCANDALOUS STREETS I, II, III
FEAR MY GANGSTA I, II, III IV, V
THESE STREETS DON'T LOVE NOBODY I, II
BURY ME A G I, II, III, IV, V
A GANGSTA'S EMPIRE I, II, III, IV
THE DOPEMAN'S BODYGAURD I II
THE REALEST KILLAZ I II III
THE LAST OF THE OGS I II III
By **Tranay Adams**

MARRIED TO A BOSS I II III
By **Destiny Skai & Chris Green**

KINGZ OF THE GAME I II III IV V VI VII
CRIME BOSS
By **Playa Ray**

FUK SHYT
By **Blakk Diamond**

DON'T F#CK WITH MY HEART I II
By **Linnea**

ADDICTED TO THE DRAMA I II III
IN THE ARM OF HIS BOSS II
By **Jamila**

YAYO I II III IV
A SHOOTER'S AMBITION I II
BRED IN THE GAME
By **S. Allen**

LOYALTY AIN'T PROMISED I II
By **Keith Williams**

TRAP GOD I II III
RICH $AVAGE I II III
MONEY IN THE GRAVE I II III
By **Martell Troublesome Bolden**

FOREVER GANGSTA I II
GLOCKS ON SATIN SHEETS I II
By **Adrian Dulan**

TOE TAGZ I II III IV
LEVELS TO THIS SHYT I II
IT'S JUST ME AND YOU
By **Ah'Million**

KINGPIN DREAMS I II III
RAN OFF ON DA PLUG
By **Paper Boi Rari**

CONFESSIONS OF A GANGSTA I II III IV
CONFESSIONS OF A JACKBOY I II
By **Nicholas Lock**

I'M NOTHING WITHOUT HIS LOVE
SINS OF A THUG
TO THE THUG I LOVED BEFORE
A GANGSTA SAVED XMAS
IN A HUSTLER I TRUST
By **Monet Dragun**

QUIET MONEY I II III
THUG LIFE I II III
EXTENDED CLIP I II
A GANGSTA'S PARADISE
By **Trai'Quan**

RELENTLESS GOON | PRINCE A. TAUHID

CAUGHT UP IN THE LIFE I II III
THE STREETS NEVER LET GO I II III
By **Robert Baptiste**

NEW TO THE GAME I II III
MONEY, MURDER & MEMORIES I II III
By **Malik D. Rice**

CREAM I II III
THE STREETS WILL TALK
By **Yolanda Moore**

LIFE OF A SAVAGE I II III IV
A GANGSTA'S QUR'AN I II III IV
MURDA SEASON I II III
GANGLAND CARTEL I II III
CHI'RAQ GANGSTAS I II III IV
KILLERS ON ELM STREET I II III
JACK BOYZ N DA BRONX I II III
A DOPEBOY'S DREAM I II III
JACK BOYS VS DOPE BOYS I II III
COKE GIRLZ
COKE BOYS
SOSA GANG I II
BRONX SAVAGES
BODYMORE KINGPINS
By **Romell Tukes**

THE STREETS MADE ME I II III
By **Larry D. Wright**

CONCRETE KILLA I II III
VICIOUS LOYALTY I II III
By **Kingpen**

RELENTLESS GOON | PRINCE A. TAUHID

THE ULTIMATE SACRIFICE I, II, III, IV, V, VI
KHADIFI
IF YOU CROSS ME ONCE I II
ANGEL I II III IV
IN THE BLINK OF AN EYE
By **Anthony Fields**

THE LIFE OF A HOOD STAR
By **Ca$h & Rashia Wilson**

THE STREETS WILL NEVER CLOSE I II III
By **K'ajji**

NIGHTMARES OF A HUSTLA I II III
By **King Dream**

HARD AND RUTHLESS I II
MOB TOWN 251
THE BILLIONAIRE BENTLEYS I II III
REAL G'S MOVE IN SILENCE
By **Von Diesel**

GHOST MOB
By **Stilloan Robinson**

MOB TIES I II III IV V VI
SOUL OF A HUSTLER, HEART OF A KILLER I II
GORILLAZ IN THE TRENCHES
By **SayNoMore**

BODYMORE MURDERLAND I II III
THE BIRTH OF A GANGSTER I II
By **Delmont Player**

221

RELENTLESS GOON | PRINCE A. TAUHID

FOR THE LOVE OF A BOSS
By **C. D. Blue**

KILLA KOUNTY I II III IV
By Khufu

MOBBED UP I II III IV
THE BRICK MAN I II III IV V
THE COCAINE PRINCESS I II III IV V VI VII
By **King Rio**

MONEY GAME I II
By **Smoove Dolla**

A GANGSTA'S KARMA I II III
By **FLAME**

KING OF THE TRENCHES I II III
By **GHOST & TRANAY ADAMS**

QUEEN OF THE ZOO I II
By **Black Migo**

GRIMEY WAYS I II III
By **Ray Vinci**

XMAS WITH AN ATL SHOOTER
By **Ca$h & Destiny Skai**

KING KILLA
By **Vincent "Vitto" Holloway**

BETRAYAL OF A THUG I II
By **Fre$h**

RELENTLESS GOON | PRINCE A. TAUHID

THE MURDER QUEENS I II
By **Michael Gallon**

TREAL LOVE
By **Le'Monica Jackson**

FOR THE LOVE OF BLOOD I II
By **Jamel Mitchell**

HOOD CONSIGLIERE I II
By **Keese**

PROTÉGÉ OF A LEGEND I II
LOVE IN THE TRENCHES
By **Corey Robinson**

BORN IN THE GRAVE I II III
By **Self Made Tay**

MOAN IN MY MOUTH
By **XTASY**

TORN BETWEEN A GANGSTER AND A
GENTLEMAN
By **J-BLUNT & Miss Kim**

LOYALTY IS EVERYTHING I II
By **Molotti**

HERE TODAY GONE TOMORROW
By **Fly Rock**

PILLOW PRINCESS
By **S. Hawkins**

RELENTLESS GOON | PRINCE A. TAUHID

SANCTIFIED AND HORNY
by **XTASY**

THE PLUG OF LIL MEXICO 2
by **CHRIS GREEN**

THE BLACK DIAMOND CARTEL
by **SAYNOMORE**

THE BIRTH OF A GANGSTER 3
by **DELMONT PLAYER**

RELENTLESS GOON | PRINCE A. TAUHID

BOOKS BY LDP'S CEO, CA$H

TRUST IN NO MAN
TRUST IN NO MAN 2
TRUST IN NO MAN 3
BONDED BY BLOOD
SHORTY GOT A THUG
THUGS CRY
THUGS CRY 2
THUGS CRY 3
TRUST NO BITCH
TRUST NO BITCH 2
TRUST NO BITCH 3
TIL MY CASKET DROPS
RESTRAINING ORDER
RESTRAINING ORDER 2
IN LOVE WITH A CONVICT
LIFE OF A HOOD STAR
XMAS WITH AN ATL SHOOTER

www.ingramcontent.com/pod-product-compliance
Lightning Source LLC
Chambersburg PA
CBHW071153260626
47162CB00003B/1033